Pink Paisley Scarf

A Contemporary Novel

Marylu Downing

Library of Congress Control number:
ISBN number: **978-1-962243-07-0**

Cover painting: Marylu Downing.
Cover designer: Sadira Attebery

All Poems attributed to Hafiz, Rumi etc. are in the public domain.

moonvinesbooks.com
PO Box 2674
Avila Beach CA 93424

I wish I could show you

when you are lonely or in darkness,

the astonishing light

of your own being.

Hafez

Table of Contents

To lovers who must decide.
To a spicy cake imbued with the power of love.
To those working to save places from destruction.
To dreamers who weave words, stitch together imagined worlds.

Prologue

Deirdre unhooked her water bottle and took a long, tepid drink. Mateo had told her to keep walking toward the row of trees, and through them, she would see ruins.

The sunburn from yesterday was peeling now, and she resisted the urge to scratch her face and arms. Stepping over a lizard, she came closer to the tall trees. She saw the chunky quarried rock piled up very high, then adobe walls, and above it all, a gargoyle-like creature with bulging eyes. Its long tongue hung out over what was left of a bathing pool, now just a muddy leaf-filled hole with a few fragments of tile and clay on the sides.

Two winged women topped the wall above the pool, their faces toward the sky. Bits of blue paint still clung to some of their feathers. *They must have been brightly painted at one time,* Deirdre thought, as she sat down by the pool, took out her notebook, and sketched the gargoyle dating it back to a time of vibrant jungle civilization: Maya, or just after the decline.

She looked up and saw vines crawling all over the back walls. Moon vine prominent, it seemed to strangle out the other plants. Deirdre wanted to see and feel what the shamans experienced when they had visions, made prophecies and collected plants that cured maladies. That's why she'd come here today.

If Mateo were here, he might smile at her again in that charming way he had and say, "Ancient peoples." But right now, she was glad to be on her own as she explored this maze with birds' nests tucked into stone walls. The first bird she saw was small, brown, and unremarkable until it ruffled its feathers and flashed shiny coppery metallic.

Around the corner, a large pottery head lay underneath thick, knotted wooden trunks of old vines. The head with wide-open eyes, and parted lips, almost forming an "O". Deirdre saw no indication that it had smashed through rows of tile. "They wanted her here," she said out loud.

She imagined rituals accompanied by something bitter and intoxicating, like this moon plant, something to be worshiped itself because it made you feel you'd transcended the earthly. With a shaman's help, she had tried it once.

Deirdre went on walking toward a huge tree filled with yellow trumpet-shaped flowers, larger than any datura she'd ever seen. The flowers pulled limbs down until the blossoms swept the ground. The locals said that fragrant *Devil's Snare* could be used for a powerful trip but often caused temporary blindness. She didn't want to risk anything like that. So many ritual plants held danger. Plants could be toxic, or they could cure sickness, someone knowledgeable must be consulted.

She walked on toward another tangle of vines with yet more trumpet-shaped flowers in shades of red and orange and heard the buzzing of a million wings; pollinators at work. Hundreds of swallowtails, blue sulfurs, big fat bouncy bees, and bright orange butterflies, maybe Mexican silverspots. This was a place where insects thrived without fear of pesticides. As she got closer, she saw that the flowers had long stamens. Very sexy. No wonder the bees were going crazy. She worried a little about how aroused she felt right now. Her moods were intense and could rapidly shift. The adrenaline charge of stepping into new terrain, with luscious things to unveil, is what she craved.

She cut moon vine pods and tucked them into her pouch. Inside the coolness of thick walls, she focused on inscriptions carved into columns. Fancy pictographs. She knew how to read most of this language. She took a few sips from the vine tea she'd brought with her and lay down on the warm tile floor, nesting her hair in a soft pile of leaves.

Before she closed her eyes, she saw that the sun was skimming the tops of the trees. She and Mateo would be walking back at twilight. She watched the brown bird fly out of its nest and

2

dive for one of the butterflies hovering just above the vines. Deirdre took several deep breaths and felt her body relax. She didn't know why, but she laughed and laughed again and again, the sounds echoing off the courtyard walls. Even though she was alone in this strange place, she didn't feel lonely. It all seemed just right, and she was completely unafraid. She felt like someone who had helped invent the world at the beginning of time.

Chapter 1
Pale Wrists, Red Roses in the Desert

From a distance, Sean saw what looked like a mannequin, stiff white limbs akimbo, lying beside the road. But what would a mannequin be doing here in the middle of nowhere? There was no department store for 15 miles or more. Nothing but scrub brush, packs of coyotes, tales of UFO sightings, and ghostly desert ships.

As he got closer, Sean clamped his hands down hard on the brakes, bringing his Qlink to a stop. From his seat, he could see that this wasn't a mannequin but a woman, pale, blond, about 30 years old or so, and naked except for something tangled and clutched in one hand. When he looked closer, he saw she had a faint tattoo of roses just above her bare breasts. She must have been here a short time; there was no sunburn, and no animals had come to call on her.

He hesitated to touch her, but he wanted to see if she was injured or if she was even alive. He checked her carotid artery, and there was a very faint pulse. Her breathing was very shallow.

"What the hell happened!" he said out loud. Her body showed no sign of injury, but something had knocked her out. He got out his phone and punched in 911.

He waited, listening to the phone ring, unsure what he should say. He knew he was placing himself in jeopardy. He'd been accused of a felony once a long time ago. *But what the hell,* he thought, *that was a stupid kind of kid thing too.* He reassured himself that he really had nothing to lose here and he needed to get this young woman help right away. Her breathing was so faint that her chest, with its small white breasts, barely moved. It was a hot day, the dry hills behind him shimmering and a mirage of water on the road ahead. But this woman was no vision; she was real.

After giving all the details to the dispatcher, he clicked off his cell phone, picked up her limp arm, and took her hand. As he

4

rubbed her hand between his two large, tanned hands, he noticed a small incision, no bigger than a pinprick, on the inside of her left wrist. It showed slightly purple against her nearly bloodless white skin. He picked up her other hand and tried to get some blood flow to that arm, and there it was again, another one--a matching incision on her wrist. Too small for a suicide attempt and not enough holes for a snake bite. She didn't look like the kind to be an addict. She had no tracks down her arms or anywhere else.

"What happened here," he said softly to her, even though he knew she probably could not hear anything.

He quickly walked back to his motorcycle and took a jacket out of his pack, and tossed it over her. It was warm out, but maybe she needed shade, maybe more warmth; she looked like she was in shock. Anyway, she was naked, and it just seemed the right thing to do.

Sirens wailed in the late afternoon desert air, bouncing off the rocky slopes and the prickly pear cactus. Here they come. He figured it was still at least 10 minutes away. "Hurry it up people!" Sean shouted into the desert air. The pale blond woman was still breathing, so there was nothing for him to do but watch over her and wait for the EMTs to come and do their job--hook her up to oxygen and start a drip.

He thought of Afghanistan. He'd hated his stint as a Marine, but it had cured him of some terrible habits and he'd lost his taste for trouble. Being a Marine had scarred him, though, both inside and out. The price he'd paid for having his life saved in other ways. He'd seen some really bad stuff, including the behavior of his Marine Corps buddies. There were also the guys in the hospital, just a mess. And worse, the kids, missing arms and legs. The whole experience had made him want nothing more to do with the military once he finished his commitment. Soldiers could be heroic, but on the whole, they brought a lot of suffering to the very people they were there to protect. He had his own wounds, real ones, as a permanent souvenir. His headaches and a bad memory. Shrapnel from hidden explosives added to his normal jumpiness.

A condition he'd had since he was a very young kid, even before he'd been removed to a foster family, the one that gave him a real life.

Damn, they're taking their time! He listened to the sirens coming closer.

The blond woman's breathing had changed; it sounded a little deeper, with rough sighing in between breaths. He wasn't sure this was a good sign. He was really worried about her, and his hands shook a little. He watched her carefully. The exertion of each breath seemed to tax her; her whole body rose with each breath, sinking back down into the warm asphalt road as she exhaled. Kind of like how he felt when he had an asthma attack. He began massaging her limbs again, even though he worried about the police knowing he had touched the woman.

Finally, help arrived, two deputies in a squad car from the Palmdale Sheriff's Department. He stood up and walked over to the car.

"Hi, glad to see you guys, this gal needs help. I only took her pulse and tossed my jacket over her, but otherwise, she's just like I found her. I can't figure out what's happened to her. Funny, at first I thought she was a mannequin."

"Nothing funny about any of this from the looks of it, sir," the Deputy said, putting on his hat. "Get a blanket, Cindy, and give that jacket to him!" he yelled to the round woman with long black hair. "You know you've left some of your DNA now, sir, and it may confuse our test results," the Sheriff practically shouted. *Oh man,* Sean thought, so *much for being a good Samaritan.*

The Deputy, Cindy, got out of the car and ran over to the pale blond. Pulling Sean's jacket off, she tossed a thermal blanket over the woman. More sirens. In minutes a white ambulance, shining in the sun, pulled in with medics who swung the back doors open. Two guys got out the stretcher. As they ran over to her, the male Deputy stopped them.

"Wait, we need a couple of pictures before you take her." Cindy came over and took the blanket back into her arms while the

6

other one, the Deputy who seemed to be giving all the orders, got out a small digital camera and snapped away. Finished, he walked toward Sean.

"Hi, I'm Deputy Vargas," the man said, extending his hand to Sean. "What's your name and address, sir?" he asked, and then as if an afterthought, "And your driver's license."

"Sean, sir, Sean Quinlin and I'm staying here in Pear Blossom. Here's my license, sir."

"Know this young lady?" the Sheriff said, getting out a recording device as small as an iPhone.

"No, never saw her before and don't know her."

He watched an EMT pry the pink scarf from the woman's fingers and hand it to deputy Cindy, who put it into a plastic bag, attached a tag to it, and placed it on the back seat of the squad car. The EMTs hurriedly tucked the woman into blankets on the gurney stretcher and lifted her into the ambulance.

The sun was pretty high in a clear sky now; it was going to be a star-filled night again. *Even though Antelope Valley was getting overcrowded, off this Pear Blossom exit, you still had a pretty good view of the sky,* Sean thought. And the sunsets, sometimes affected by L. A. smog over the hills, were filled with oranges and a purples like the clear glass his grandmother used to leave out in the desert sun to color.

He barely remembered his grandmother. She was Chumash and Paiute, and barely spoke English. The sirens started up as the ambulance screeched back onto the highway. Sean heard the Sheriff say again, "You actually thought this was a mannequin sir?"

"Yes, she didn't look real to me from a distance." He knew he'd have to explain his arrest record, but he wasn't too worried about that. He'd convinced himself that it wouldn't amount to much, seeing as how he'd called for help for this young woman. "Oh, and here's this," Sean said as he handed Sheriff Deputy Vargas his VA card. They'd know he'd done service, and cops were usually sympathetic to Marines with an honorable discharge.

"Thanks, Sean Quinlin. Thank you for your service," Vargas said, handing the card back.

Sean was still puzzled about those purple pinpricks. Possibly IVs or other medical procedures? He thought about mentioning her wrists, the pinprick incisions, to Vargas, but decided it would be better to say nothing.

"No ID on the lady. No purse around," Deputy Vargas said into a recording device.

He continued, "Found by one Sean Quinlin at 10:15, nearest town, Pear Blossom."

"Well, Mr. Quinlin, you'll need to follow us in to Palmdale and give us a statement.."

"I know, I know," Sean said, nodding towards his small cheap motorcycle. "I won't be able to go that fast; my engine is small and has some problems right now."

"Oh man, just come with us; we'll take you in the squad car and bring you back here later for the bike. Just tuck it beyond the highway into the brush over there and remember where it is, so you'll be good to go when you get dropped off. People drive this stretch so fast that they won't even notice it. And don't worry; we don't really care about your engine size!"

This made both men laugh, even though Sean laughed cautiously. Deputy Cindy turned and got back into the car. Sean knew that she would be the one to have to return him here later. He wondered if his big build, and his dark tattoos intimidated her, and then he decided she'd seen it all before.

Sean thought to himself, *Why me? Why did I have to be the first person to see this woman and stop?* Maybe others had just driven by, but how could you ignore a naked blond with a pink scarf lying near the road? What the hell, maybe he'd saved her life, but it hadn't taken much on his part. A simple 911 phone call. Maybe if his motorcycle had gone faster, he might not have stopped. He couldn't quit thinking about her, about her ghostly face, so serene looking, but her torso and limbs thin and long. *What the hell was this woman's story?* he wondered.

By accident, the bag with the scarf slid out the door when it was opened for him. Sean didn't bother to say anything. He would retrieve it later. He had good instincts. When you mix Irish with Indian, you could spot every hawk on the horizon and could cover any mishap with a wild story.

Chapter 2
The Jewel of India

Elizabeth wrapped her favorite pashmina around her neck and over her silk blouse. She loved the elaborate paisley design in swirling lines of silver and deeper shades of rose. She always thought the paisleys looked like tadpoles, with their fat bellies and little tails, or like teardrops. Or lately, as she thought about it more, droplets of sperm.

Her lover, ViJay, had told her that this simple little paisley motif held within it an entire religious thought, a belief in life eternal. ViJay, tall and dark, East Indian, knew even more about textiles than she did. He had also taught her about sex and how to make real love, slow and sensuous. He had given her the *Kama Sutra* with hand-colored illustrations. What she hadn't expected was that the book was a manual for sustaining love. Love, something that repeatedly seemed to slip away from Elizabeth. But, even after five years, ViJay still haunted her, and she wondered if she could ever release the hold he had on her.

Tonight was a new start. She had agreed to meet up with a guy she'd been emailing via eHarmony.com. They would have dinner together. She was wearing the scarf as a small comfort, like the transitional objects kids carry on their first day of kindergarten.

She sat down on her worn loveseat to pull on her boots. Then she tugged on her cocoa-colored leather jacket, zipped it up, and got out gloves. She took one last look in the mirror, jamming unruly ginger-colored hair into her new helmet. She hoped tonight's date wouldn't be just another in what had turned out to be a long line of internet duds. At least she would get to enjoy a spicy meal in one of her favorite San Francisco restaurants. And he'd said in his email she'd be his guest for dinner. Generosity, a good sign. His name, Najid, pleased her; her love for all things from the Orient was still strong. The colors and flavors, the tales and

10

especially the textiles of the former Silk Road lured her in. Maybe, too, Elizabeth secretly hoped Najid would be a bit like ViJay, but then, that was reaching for the moon. She felt very lonely right now. With her parents both dead and having recently lost the rock of her life, her grandmother, she only had her sister to count on. But her sister was always off on a botanical hunt of some kind and gone from California for months at a time.

After she locked the front door of her flat, she pulled on the gloves. On her Vespa, she opened the choke and waited for a count of 30 and then kick-started the engine and drove off toward The Jewel of India, where a curried meal, and perhaps, a hot date, awaited.

She hadn't had a date for months. Not since she'd called the police on the last internet guy she'd met. He turned aggressive and mean. Once she figured out he was crazy, she told him never to call her again. That's when he started stalking her. And the guy before him. Oh stop it! Her mind was busy when it should be getting calm, and ready for a great night out.

The wasp-like buzz of her Vespa drowned out any other thoughts as she drove up and down hills, from one hilltop where she saw lights on the Bay Bridge and from another, the tops of the terra cotta Golden Gate Bridge. She was energized by this brisk and slightly breezy ride across town on a star-sprinkled San Francisco evening.

She pulled up in front of The Jewel of India and put down the kickstand. As she cut the engine and unsnapped her helmet, a young man in a dark uniform said, rather more loudly than he needed to, "You've got to move, can't park here. Valet parking only." She calmly fastened her helmet to the Vespa, took off her riding gloves and tucked them into the little compartment behind the seat, and locked it. "I can move it over there to where it says, 'Motorcycles only.'"

He frowned as he looked at her little motorized scooter, certainly not a candidate for a Hell's Angel, and then said, "Okay. No need to leave your keys," sending her off with a wave of his hand. She noticed he was short, dictatorial, and smelled of pot. She wheeled her bike over, locked it, and tucked the keys into her inner zip pocket with her license and a credit card. She hoped she'd find Najid right away and that he would not stand her up. Nothing had been going right lately, and she just wanted this evening to work out.

When the door to the restaurant was opened for her, she breathed in rich, nose-tickling scents. Smoky steam from a sizzling tandoori dish curled up from a waiter's hands. It took a minute for the steam to die back as she looked for "a guy in a powder blue jacket." He was to look for "a redhead." Each had pictures from eHarmony.com to help them recognize each other. She felt her teeth sticking to her lips, a smile frozen on her face. Her hands shook a little, and she realized that she was more nervous than she thought. She tucked both hands into her jacket pockets and felt a half-used cough drop in its sticky paper.

Elizabeth decided to search for powder blue and hoped that not too many men would be wearing what seemed a popular color now for men's blazers. She associated powder blue blazers with pictures of her father from the 1960s. She wasn't too fond of the look.

The place was full and loud with happy chatter. She saw someone waving at her. A George Clooney look-alike, darker but with the same square jaw and thick arched eyebrows and sporting the jacket described in his email, stood up at a table for two, not far from the front door. He seemed eager. She noticed again how handsome he was. In person, he was much more striking than in the picture he'd posted. She wondered if he had downplayed his good looks on purpose. Of course, she'd chosen a really good picture of herself, which minimized her sharp chin and the wildness of her hair.

She held out her cool hand to Mr. Clooney. "Najid?"

"Ah, you know how to say my name. Thank you. Yes, it's a pleasure, Elizabeth," he said, giving her a two-handed shake. He stepped in front of her to pull out her chair. Good manners, she

12

noted. Not always part of the modern dating scene. She liked that he seemed a bit old-fashioned, but she understood that he was also from another culture, maybe trained to treat women this way.

She unzipped her leather jacket, and slid her arms free, but before she had time to hang it over the back of her chair, a waiter in a turban came over and took it from her. "Take the scarf, too?" he asked.

"No, not the scarf." she answered. He nodded and left with her jacket. Suddenly she was aware of the restaurant. Everything about the place seemed exotic, yet familiar. The waiters with their Punjabi white jackets, embroidered in more white, their shimmering sashed pants, full at the top and in the leg, and then tight at the ankles and turbans wrapping their heads. The few women working there wore elaborately embroidered tops, with skirts over more skirts.

She sat down and picked up the cloth napkin and placed it on her lap. A waiter came and, without asking, poured mint tea from a long-necked brass teapot. Najid picked up a menu and handed it across the table to her.

"I'm very familiar with these dishes; if you want, I can just order, and we can share, or you pick one of your favorites. I hope you don't mind; I've already ordered an appetizer of samosas."

She smiled and said, "Well, that sounds great to me." She loosened her scarf and re-adjusted it. She set the menu down and took a sip of the very hot tea to make her lips let go of her teeth. "I mean, all of it sounds fine, sharing, and I love samosas. Thank you." Already she was stumbling with her words.

"Beautiful paisley scarf." He reached over to touch it, and instinctively, she pulled back and sat up straight. Wary, she was protective of her private space.

Sitting back and putting his hand in his lap, he asked, "Is it from India or Scotland?"

Paisley, that combination of dots, swirls, and sensual curving lines outlined by more flowing lines. The Persians, then the Scots. She had to stop herself from going down a long line of

13

explanations stemming from her research in Asian History and her flailing attempt at graduate school. Instead, she took another sip of tea.

"Well, it says 'made in India' on the label," Elizabeth finally answered, "but I think it was purchased in Pakistan." She didn't want to say too much right now about dropping out of school recently because Sanskrit overwhelmed her, how grandmother's illness consumed her time, and that she was definitely not going to say anything about the man who gave her this scarf five years ago—her lost lover, ViJay.

A waiter came with a tray of samosas and an orange-colored tamarind dipping sauce. "Oh, these look so good," Elizabeth said, "And I'm starving!" she said as she lifted one fat round samosa from the tray and spooned some sauce onto the small plate before her. He laughed, and she realized he must find her amusing. Better ask, she thought.

"Uh oh, did I do something wrong?"

"No, not at all. It's just that I'm used to the serious women of Tehran. I like your direct qualities. I call myself Persian," he added. "When we talk with each other my family and I don't ever say Iranian. Just Persian. Please excuse me for laughing."

He seemed a strange combination of formal, old-fashioned, and unexpectedly direct.

"I know something of Persia," she said, "I've researched that area for my thesis on the textiles and designs of Iran, and Turkey and how the trade along the Silk Road influenced the artisans."

Oh no, she thought, *she could sound so professorial at times.* And all she really wanted was to eat well, maybe have sex, and forget all about her Ph.D. thesis.

"Fantastic," he said, carefully dipping an into the sauce. "Then you will have to tell me all about it."

Elizabeth was in the middle of a bite of the tangy samosa, so her date chimed in.

"Did you know the samosa is first from my country, Iran, and it was made for men to put into their saddle bags as a snack?" Elizabeth raised her eyebrows at his comment, swallowed, and then answered,

"I have never been to the Middle East, but I lived in Pakistan and then in Delhi for a year. Once as part of a college project. I had to carve one of those wood printing blocks for a textiles class. It was a lot harder than I thought it would be, and I ended up chipping off a few parts of the design." She laughed at the memory. He laughed, too and nodded in agreement.

She looked at her date and smiled. His dark eyes and burnished skin. *Uh oh, here I go again,* she thought.

"I'm glad you know paisley," he said, "the design has special meaning for me. Are you familiar with Zoroaster?"

"Well, I know just a little about Zoroaster and his ideas and how the paisley design has a special meaning, but what I'm thinking about now is how delicious these samosas are," Elizabeth took another from the tray and tried to change the topic to something lighter, even though she realized that she wasn't dealing with an ordinary man. His knowledge, his manner, and his looks all appealed to her.

She already knew she would end up ordering the sizzling tandoori chicken and some naan, just the plain kind without garlic or cheese. She had just gone from being a total vegetarian when her Dr. suggested adding "just a little protein" into her diet, and now she had become used to chewing chicken and looking for the small bones that could hide in fish dishes. Still, she missed eating lamb more than any other meat.

She had to admit that even though she had an aversion to men wearing powder blue, he looked good in it. She noticed too, a little gray showing in his thick head of charcoal hair.

"This scent always takes me back to New Delhi and Kolkata," Elizabeth said as the yellow dal was set before each of them. She picked up the bowl with her hands and took a sip. "Just right," she said, "not too thick or over-seasoned." Her date nodded in agreement

"Ummmm," she said without thinking.

He looked at her as he sipped from his bowl and smiled.

"How was your time there, in those two places?" he asked.

"It was magnificent, although when not speaking English, I found it hard to communicate."

"Oh yes, there are over a hundred languages, twenty-two official, but many people know some English," Najid said, taking another big sip and finishing his cup of dal.

"I tried to at least get some sense of Hindi and of Bengali. But then, in Pakistan, it was Urdu and Punjabi. I used to mangle all of them." Elizabeth said, looking over at him.

Najid nodded as though he understood. "Being Persian, we speak Farsi and some older versions of Persian, but everyone knows English too, especially in my family of traders. We have to."

"Najid, I'm very interested in Persia, the history, so old and rich. You can probably tell me a lot."

"Well, Rumi says: 'Seek the wisdom that will untie your knot. Seek the path that demands your whole being'." He looked over at her as if to say, *let's go deep*. She felt very fidgety, but also, for some reason, this Rumi quote almost brought her to tears. Rumi was so popular in America now, and she could see why. Rumi could define something so succinctly yet say it in a way that cut into you.

"Those Rumi lines seem meant just for me." She looked at him, noticing that his brown eyes were flecked with green.

Happily, the food they'd ordered arrived. Platters steamed and gave off aromas of spice and of the East. "I'm glad," he said, starting to dig into his lamb, and then he offered her a bite. She took the lamb and never mentioned that she'd given it up.

She couldn't pass the hot tandoori platter, so she sliced some chicken and spooned it, with the curled onion and peppers, onto an extra plate the waiter had brought.

Already sharing a meal, really sharing it. But she'd always been suspicious about men, or women for that matter, who could quote poetry. She suspected that they took these smoothly put-together words to use whenever they might not have something original to say.

They went back to safer topics, their favorite restaurants, and their special places to hike in the area, and then they each ordered a beer. The light brew made her just a little more relaxed, and more talkative. He seemed so put-together and clean, and, well, handsome, was all she could think.

Najid kept wanting to hold her hand, reaching out and then pulling back, until finally she relented and reached across to him. She wanted to mention her interest in the boy warrior of Persia but thought better of it. That would be for later. She was already jumping to later, another time, another date.

Their meal finished, the evening coming to a close, Najid said, "On the dating site, you said you were looking for a man to take hikes with, to have serious conversations about books and movies, but you didn't say anything about a 'long term relationship.'"

Elizabeth felt her face flush, and she just felt a little trapped as she replied, "Yes, that's right," and then, to relieve the tension, she laughed. But, Najid did not. He just kept looking over at her, holding her hand and smiling. She thought she pleased him, but wasn't sure why.

"Okay, I see that makes you uncomfortable, but just to be honest, I am hoping to find someone who will come to have great meaning to me, and who will want to share more than bites." Najid squeezed her hand and continued. " 'Life is short as a half-taken breath, don't plant anything but love.' That is my favorite Rumi," Najid paused. "I would like very much to see you again, Elizabeth. I like you, and we could go somewhere else next time. You will pick. But I have to let you know that I do a lot of international traveling, so sometimes I am gone for a few weeks. I can let you know. What about you?"

17

"I'm not traveling, even though I wish I were. Right now, I'm doing contract work from home, graphics work, and I just started again, so I really need to build up the business." She dodged the issue, and didn't answer his question.

"What about us, though? Would you be willing to see me again, Elizabeth?"

"Yes, Najid, I would like that." She stammered a little bit and hoped it wasn't too noticeable that she was shaken by this unexpected closeness he seemed to want. But it was what she also yearned for...the sharing of a meal, conversation, all of it. And she had agreed to see him again, surprised as she heard herself say, "Yes".

He helped her get her jacket and held it out for her to put on. They walked outside together, and he watched while she retrieved her Vespa, snapped her helmet closed, and pulled on driving gloves. She waved goodbye as he laughed and waved back. She whirred off into the night, a bit of her pink scarf fluttering behind.

They didn't kiss, but he had hugged her, and she smelled the faintest odor of sandalwood as she climbed the hills toward home.

Chapter 3
Pink Paisley Scarf

Small town, desert heat permeating everything, every memory, Palmdale. He hadn't expected to stay, but the blond woman with her pale wrists and strange marks had hooked him. He couldn't let go of the image in his mind—her lying naked by the road, pale scarf in her hand, roses tattooed above her breasts.

He pushed his sleeping bag down so he could reach into his jeans pocket to pull out his vibrating cell phone.

"What, what, sorry I can hardly hear you. Yes, I'm Sean. Yes, I can hear you now. So this is Deputy Vargas from yesterday, right?" Sean turned up the volume. "You say you can't ID her? I'm sorry, I'm really having trouble hearing you. I'll swing by the hospital a little later."

"No, come by the department at 10:30 this morning."

Deputy Vargas insisted, and Sean would comply.

Sean pushed all the way out of his bag now and pulled on his white T-shirt with the mountain goat on the front—Capricorn. His foster sister had given it to him the last time he rolled through town, before she moved north.

He wondered why the Sheriff's office didn't just fingerprint the blond, but sometimes, especially if it's a sex ring, they sand off the fingertips, or use acid. What people are capable of; he'd seen it all. Then he thought, the deputies probably had too.

And I've got her scarf, he thought to himself, shaking his head. Oh yes, Deputy Cindy had bagged it, but it had slid from the car seat when she'd opened the door for Sean. Later that afternoon, when she'd dropped him off and sped back onto the highway, he went over and picked up the zip-locked bag from where the wind had blown it on the ground next to some tumbleweed. He'd opened up the bag and examined the scarf, thin wool material, and, if he wasn't mistaken, paisley print, most likely from Pakistan or India.

19

For a few weeks, Sean had been posted in Pakistan to guard State Department officials.

He thought for a minute about bringing the bag with the scarf in with him today, but that might require too much explaining, and it might seem to make him more of a suspect. No, he'd keep it for now. He stuck the baggie in his jacket pocket.

Yesterday when he called the hospital, he'd been told that the woman was still sleeping, not quite in a coma, but she hadn't been able to form any coherent words yet. Even so, he hoped to see her later today.

He took some water, poured it into his hand, and smoothed down his straight dark hair as best he could. Being here in Palmdale rekindled an adventure he'd always thought about taking. He was going to do some investigation of his own. He'd always wanted to hike back into the hills, and this time of the year, early spring, was the time to do it. He might even hike into a little snow. What he was after was the phantom ship, the galleon that was rumored to be drying out near Palma Seca, what they always called Indian Springs when he was a kid living here with his foster family.

He folded his tiny tent and rolled everything into a neat pack which he carefully tucked and tied onto his Qlink saddlebags. He tugged on his heavy boots and put on his helmet before kick starting his little motorcycle and heading up the road to Deputy Vargas. Afterward he planned to head to the nearby Palmdale Medical Center, where that pale young woman lay in ICU. He'd look up the address on his phone just to make sure the Center hadn't moved from where he remembered it. His memory was not always reliable now. Being blown up, every part of his body suffered for a while.

This whole landscape was lying on top of lakes of water. As he drove on past Joshua trees, past scrub oak, and a few early blooming California poppies, he thought about the ship. It was rumored to have sailed into the Salton Sea—the sea saltier than the Pacific Ocean. Why couldn't a ship have wandered here? Why not? It's California, the land of myth-making and Hollywood and earthquakes and fire. Seas once covered the whole place. He had fossil rocks with shells to prove it too.

Sean arrived at the Sheriff's office exactly at 10:30. The military had really trained him to pay attention to time.

Sean noticed how short and square the Deputy was. Sean had seen a guy just like him, same build and the same staccato style of talking. It was at a 4-Square Revival in Palmdale, with his foster sister, Abigail, when he was a teenager. A big tent, 102 degrees outside and almost as hot inside. The minister was sweating and, in a religious frenzy, spewing spit into the air with each enthusiastic burst of speech. Sean couldn't take him seriously, not because of the sweat and spit, but because this guy kept referring to "God's Decycles" instead of disciples and "All of God's Peekles." "The Templer of God." "The last Stupper of Jesus and his 12 Decycles." So many funny mispronunciations he took one look at his foster sister, Abby, and had to go outside to laugh like crazy. That was the last time he let anyone talk him into anything having to do with the church.

"Are you sure you didn't move the body?" Sean shook off the memory of the 4-Square revival and tried to concentrate on answering the Deputy Sheriff. He felt himself breaking into a sweat and felt his face go red. Both signaled that his infamous temper was about to flair. He didn't want to lose it; that temper had gotten him into a lot of trouble in the past. He took a deep breath and answered Deputy Vargas.

"No, I did not; I didn't move her, sir, all I did was check her pulse, and then I simply took my jacket and placed it over her. It was hot as hell, and she didn't need warming up, but she didn't have anything on. I thought she might be going into shock. The only thing on her body was a scarf wrapped in her hand.

"Scarf?

"Pink, I saw your associate, Cindy, put it in the squad car." Sean squirmed a little. It wasn't a lie exactly, well, maybe one of omission. He still had the scarf. He wanted to give it to that blond.

It was almost a mission. He had to do it; he felt compelled to. He guessed he wanted to see her, talk to her, really know she was okay.

Deputy Vargas put his notes down on the polished mahogany desk, reached into his pocket and brought out a handkerchief, and proceeded to blow his nose. "You know she's not at the hospital any longer so we can't really get any more information about her. We did fingerprint her finally, and so we are checking against recorded prints, but otherwise, we know nothing other than her cousin's name. We feel the case will be closed soon, but we may talk to you again if we need to."

"She's okay? She's been released already? Her cousin?" Sean was incredulous. He'd seen so many messed up people, so many wrecked bodies, and he couldn't believe that in one day's time, she'd been good enough to leave the hospital. She had been unconscious, barely a pulse.

"That's right. When she came out of the coma, she asked for a phone. Another tall woman, another blond, came in later. She checked in at the desk, and then no one ever saw her or the other woman leave the hospital, but they did. At least the woman, we only have her first name, was able to remember who she was and a phone number. She was able to get someone to come and get her, without our permission, of course. It's like she's on the run or something. Okay, that's all pal; we don't need anything more from you right now." Deputy Vargas turned away from the desk, away from Sean, and walked down the hallway. Sean had been dismissed.

Now how would he ever find her? But Vargas said her cousin had signed her out. He would stay in town and try to get some information. In the meantime, he would go to the hospital and sniff around, pretend he didn't know she was released yet, and see if he could get anything, especially a name. He could do it. He knew he had his ways. And he had her scarf.

Chapter 4
A Letter, A Bouquet, An Incident

Elizabeth held her morning coffee in one hand and Najid's letter in the other. She sat outside in the slightly rickety Adirondack chair that she had painted mauve on a dull gray San Francisco day. It was after she quit graduate school and was flailing about, wondering how to fill her time. Her small narrow flat came with a tiny garden, and she used it as much as possible.

She sipped from the mug of very strong coffee and took a second look at Najid's letter.

Elizabeth was surprised and touched that Najid had taken the time to write and actually mail a letter to her. Najid had used the old-fashioned thin blue paper, the kind that used to be specifically for airmail because it was lighter and the postage would be less. This fragile paper in her hands felt like a captured moth trying to escape a clumsy, sweating hand. He'd probably grown up writing letters on that airmail paper. He'd told her when he'd called her right after that first dinner that his cousins had to flee Iran, and quickly, but still, they'd kept in touch by regular mail for the years before everyone had the internet and Skype and Facetime.

"I just couldn't stop thinking about you on your Vespa, pink scarf trailing behind you in the dark like a flag," he wrote. She hoped he was not going to stalk her aggressively like that last guy, but Najid seemed different, old-fashioned, and trustworthy. Still, ah yes, the silver-tongued thing. Elizabeth was always a sucker for a guy who could do romantic talk. But then he offered depth too. She remembered their long conversation over steaming curry about the "Cradle of Civilization." Of course, at her age, nearing 40, she was more interested in a real cradle holding a real baby.

Uncrossing her legs, she stretched. Yesterday for the first time in a month, the first time since her spill, she had gotten out her mountain bike and taken a ride over the Golden Gate Bridge into Marin county and onto the trails of Mt. Tamalpais. So used to the insistent sound of her Vespa's motor, the quiet bicycle allowed her to hear songbirds, the wind kicking up whitecaps in Richardson Bay. The ride had been just what Elizabeth needed. She was wound up tightly these days, trying to build her graphics business, self-doubt, and longing for sexual pleasure.

Elizabeth finished her coffee, folded the note, and slipped it back into the envelope. He had promised to call her, but she hadn't heard from him. Only this one letter, short and certainly sweet. It ended with "I miss you. The sunsets here make me think of you."

When she got up from the chair and walked the steps back into her flat, her calf muscles screamed at her. She opened her backpack and got out Arnica gel. As she rubbed in the last of the gel, she noticed her thesis, just where she'd tossed it months ago on the end of the kitchen table. The thesis, now sporting drops of coffee and grease, was a grim reminder of her recent decision to drop out of a prestigious Ph.D. program. She kicked herself mentally for the great disrespect she was showing this now-despised thing. The title, "Orientalism and the Influence of Religious Thought on Fashion Designs," jumped out at her and seemed not only superfluous but shallow. And not a real description of her intentions. How could she explain her fascination with design, with the history of cloth, of weaving, printing cloth, and all the different ways people had used fabrics? How the cloth often subtly indicated beliefs and styles that could lead to men and women enhancing themselves? What meaning could a little decoration have in the great scheme of things?

Friends had told her that her constant need to analyze everything was what kept her from really succeeding at anything, including a lasting love relationship. Now, whenever she talked on the phone, she noticed her doodles looking more and more like little paisleys. Flowers blooming inside circular spaces, woven arches, and lines ending in dots. Over and over again. Could it

24

possibly have to do with her yearning for the sweet smell of a baby's neck? The chubby toes of any friend's baby making her estrogen count go sky-high. The paisley's shape was like a fetus in the very early stages of life when there was still a little tail attached.

She walked to her sleeping area and picked sweaters off the bed, and rolled and tucked them into the big basket on top of her dresser. She didn't fold anymore.

She walked back to the kitchen table, lifted her thesis up, and flipped through the pages. Her grandmother had been so disappointed when Elizabeth called her to say she was dropping out of school. Granny had been footing the bill too. But still, her grandmother, proper in her bearing and her culture, had quit singing opera when she became pregnant with Elizabeth's mother. And then her mother had quit her career in architecture when she was pregnant with Elizabeth's older sister, Deirdre. A lot of quitters and all over motherhood. Even so, she wanted that too. More than any flowing black robes and fancy tri-cornered hat on her head, marching to Pomp and Circumstance in the sunlight of Berkeley's Greek Amphitheater.

Of course, a trip to South Asia, Tunisia or Morocco, or another country lush with strong color and tradition would be fantastic. Arriving home after her first trip to India and Pakistan, even California seemed dull, and the people seemed so coarse. There were marigolds in California, but even the marigolds seemed smaller and less pungent. She would go into the Mexican districts at *dia de los muertos* time. Marigolds and sugar skulls made her smile. She moved the thesis over to her desk on top of a pile of other projects she was working on. People, places, and things that needed logos, brochures, or catchy images for the internet.

Elizabeth's cell phone jangled and buzzed from the other room. She ran to grab it out of her backpack. "Hello? Hello?" Static and a bad connection. No connection. The phone rang again. "Hello, hello, can you hear me?" she asked.

"Yes, I can, and your voice makes me smile."

25

"Najid, are you home?

"Yes. When can we plan something? What about today, I hope. I really missed you."

"Well, we can plan something now, but for later." Why did she stammer every time she talked to him? He could really rattle her. "I mean, later on today. We could."

She remembered how Najid's face, dark and oval-shaped, lit up, how his expressive eyes looked at her intently, and his smile, teeth white and even. *Well*, she thought, *he didn't even seem to realize that he was so handsome. So perfect.*

She needed to shower and clean up her place, and she did need to work a little.

"Okay, let's do that. What about if we meet for a walk followed by dinner, you choose the places?" Najid said.

They were to meet in about four hours. He would come to her flat, and then their walk would include a little of Golden Gate Park until they reached the Haight-Ashbury district, and there they would turn to follow the roads that led to good food. An easy goal. Cole Valley was a good bet.

While Elizabeth was elated at the idea of seeing Najid, today's bike ride had tired her. And, somehow, the thought of getting to really know someone again, becoming intimate with a man, seemed overwhelming. She'd have to be neater and pay more attention and comb her curls a little more.

She put her phone down on the kitchen table, and walked her bike from the hallway to the back garden. She walked the pack into her study, plopped it on the floor, and then went into the kitchen to pick up newspapers and the rest of the week's kitchen mess. She would work for just a few hours and then get ready.

He had just flown a long distance, but he couldn't even wait a day to see her, and in a short time they would walk the outskirts of Golden Gate Park, and she would choose the little French place in Cole Valley for dinner. Close enough to walk home at the end of the meal. She let out a big sigh as she dried and put away the dishes. They were elaborate, flowery, and real china that her mother had picked out for her after her mother's cancer had spread. This little flat did not offer many modern conveniences; that is what she'd liked about it at first. She hardly ever needed a dishwasher anyway; she didn't really socialize much, and mostly, she ate out or picked up something at Trader Joe's. She appreciated the dishes, not only because her mother had chosen them but because they were the only ones Elizabeth had.

The word Orientalism kept chiming in her head. Harems and henna and trade routes and romanticized paintings. How the West had hijacked the traditions of Asia and twisted them into a parody of exotica. But the movement had spread the beauty and art of the Persian Empire, and that is what first got her interested in the area's history and fabrics. *Why couldn't she stick to her thesis and just finish it? Could it be that hard?*

"Arrggh," she said out loud as she moved her thesis from the top of the pile and tucked it into a folder, placing it on the shelf above her desk.

After two hours of frustrating work at the computer, she gave up and tried to figure out what she would wear tonight. Something feminine or something tight and edgy? No, more than anything else, she wanted to be comfortable. She looked in the tiny closet for her white linen shirt and wheat-colored pants. And then took out the soft leather lace-up boots, still in their box from the sale at Anthropologie, and set them by the dresser. She couldn't wear the pink scarf again, could she? It was her favorite, and he'd liked it. "Yes," she said to herself as she laid everything out on her bed. Then she flopped down on the other side of the bed and fell asleep in her clothes on top of the embroidered white silk covers. Something, if her mother were still alive, she would be sure to tease her about. So fancy and feminine.

******

A brisk knock on the front door startled her awake.

Najid! She reached over to the side table and fumbled for her cell phone. The time was 5:15. *Oh jeez, if it's him, he's early, and I'm a fool.* She jumped up, took a quick glance in the mirror, smoothed her hair, and tucked it behind her ears as she ran in bare feet to answer the door. A big bouquet of flowers sprang inside the door ahead of him, practically pushing her over. "Oh, Najid, I'm sorry I haven't even changed my clothes yet. I fell asleep." He had a quizzical smile on his lips. "Not to worry, I'm early anyway; I just couldn't wait any longer to see you." And the flowers, loaded with lilies and roses, all white.

Points, she thought to herself. *Definitely, points.*

Taking the bouquet from him, she searched high up in her cupboard for a vase. "Let me get it," he said, walking over and easily bringing down a large crystal vase, her grandmother's. Somehow it was a perfectly sophisticated fit to the white bouquet which also included delicate Baby's Breath, which her older, more scientific sister called *Gypsophila*. Elizabeth filled the vase with water and then wrestled the bouquet into place on the sideboard. Her flat was small but filled with furniture she'd inherited from her grandmother. The lilies were just starting to open out, and their dizzying scent drifted into the air. She cautiously held out the lilies, with their stamen always loaded with bright pollen that stained clothes.

Najid looked handsome in a tan shirt, dark brown pants, and a sweater. She felt intimidated, still in the first things she had thrown on that morning. At least she had kicked off her boots at the door, and there they stood, bits of dirt, grass, and leaves clinging to the soles. What could she do? He would just have to accept her as she was. Not neat and fussy but not dour and serious either. He seemed to like her. She looked at him, and he winked at her. "Don't worry, you look fine. Let's go."

"I can't go like this. I'll go change," she said. It felt slightly awkward, so intimate with him there.

"Oh, don't bother. You look great as you are."

More points, but even she knew that to be false. "Just give me one minute." He smiled and nodded as she walked over and picked up the clothes from her bed, and then disappeared into the bathroom. She needed to pee, and the sound of the urine splashing

28

down into the toilet made her grimace. She flushed the toilet before she was through, just to cover the uncomfortable sound of toilet paper being torn off. *Oh, Elizabeth,* she told herself quietly, *chill out!*

She buttoned up her white shirt, threw on the linen pants and pulled the sweater on over her messy hair. She ran a brush through her hair and applied some light makeup, and went out of the bathroom. She had to sit on her bed in order to pull on her socks and lace up the boots. He stood in the kitchen near the flowers, watching her. She could hear herself breathing and heard his breath too. She heard her mother dismissing this moment. "You're such a romantic, Elizabeth, just go back in your room and read more Jane Austen, more Kahlil Gibran." Then Mother would wave her hand back and forth in the air and laugh and light another cigarette.

Right now, as Najid opened the door for her and stood waiting, the memory of her mother faded—her mother, with her locked-up emotions and skepticism. Right at this moment, Elizabeth was just fine with being a romantic. As she looked up,, he took her hand in his and kissed her on the cheek. He then kissed her lightly on the lips as she turned toward him. She liked the way the kiss felt—tender, and his smooth lips had surprised and pleased her.

"Tell me everything about yourself, my love," Najid said as they began their walk.

"Well, where should I start? Because everything is a lot." Elizabeth said, laughing as they walked together down the street, cutting through the Haight-Ashbury neighborhood near her flat.

"Make it just the important things, what you consider defines you."

"Defines me—that sounds like I should be writing an essay." She regretted saying it once the words were out of her mouth.

Najid paused, stopped walking, and looked into her eyes. "Maybe that's not what you want right now, to tell about yourself?"

"No," Elizabeth said, "I'd rather hear about the best things you saw on this last trip." She felt relieved, not having to explain the complexities of her life. A short first marriage, a sister that seemed to have disappeared over the last years, an unnerving boyfriend that had taken MTV videos seriously and wanted to reenact them. She also couldn't tell him just yet about her Ph.D. program and how it made her physically sick when she thought about it. *Let those things unfold,* she thought; for now, she preferred the comfort of small talk.

Najid reached over to push a curl away from her face and then took the pink scarf in his hand. "This," he said, "I saw many like it, but not as beautiful, when I went to the street markets. They were made in Pakistan, or that is what the vendors told me, holding them out saying, "authentic Pakistan Paisley, buy for you wife." When I didn't stop, they shouted out after me, "For you girlfriend, you mistress! That's one thing about street markets; I've lived in America so long, I've forgotten the expectation to barter and be rude in the process," he said.

"There you go again," Elizabeth said, wanting to bite her tongue as soon as the words escaped.

"What—I annoy you?"

"No," Elizabeth said, touching his shoulder, "No, I'm sorry, not at all. I'm glad you are telling me this. Maybe I was a little annoyed thinking that my scarf is a common one, sold on every street corner. "

"Well, there are a lot of pashminas sold there...India-Pakistan last leg of my last trip. Leg, right?"

"Yes, leg," she said, laughing. "I didn't know you were going to India."

"Business required a trip there to meet with someone, and I've been to this one area many times in my work. Pakistan was for pleasure. I lived there for a time."

Just then a panhandler jostled Elizabeth.

"Spare change, lady. Looks like you would have something for me." His breath smelled of onion and booze and something else slightly metallic, something like what she smelled at her dentist's office.

"Hey," Najid said, pulling Elizabeth in close to him and giving the guy a shove. The man pushed back.

"No, it's okay Najid, I was just going to give him a dollar." She was surprised by Najid's reaction, his quick anger when this was a situation that seemed to need soothing.

"Don't give him anything," Najid said, staring at the scraggly guy. He put his arm around Elizabeth and forcefully turned her, striding away, everything about him tense and assertive. The man bellowed after them, "F-you, god damned foreigner." And then he held up his middle finger.

Najid kept walking, almost pulling her along. His gait was long and fast. She felt his hand, sweaty, tightly squeezing hers until it felt like her fingers would go numb. She hoped this uncomfortable moment wouldn't ruin their evening together, but she felt her jaws clinch in an effort not to say anything more to him. Not to lecture, not to scold. She wanted to pull her arm away. But she didn't. She realized he had a strong protective streak, and maybe that was good.

Chapter 5
Tumbling Tumbleweed

Was she released from the hospital? Sean was shocked. That woman in the desert seemed so near death, ragged breathing, unconscious when he skidded to a stop next to her. This damned desert! He hated it, but like a certain kind of old girlfriend, he kept being drawn back. Palmdale, Joshua Tree, Antelope Valley. He'd had a good foster family who raised him here, and if they still lived in the desert, maybe he'd have stayed. But, other than his family, nothing much good ever happened for him in this place. Finally, the winds and the heat and loneliness drove him to the coast. He'd only been back in this dusty tumbleweed-infested place a few days. Already he was yearning for the ocean, for the feel of a waxed board tucked under his arm or the crest of a wave holding him up.

The hallway stank of disinfectant, a particularly unpleasant smell to Sean. He'd spent too much time in hallways a lot like this one, in places all over the Middle East. Finally, he was sent to San Diego when he'd returned wounded and was recovering in a VA hospital.

At the reception desk, he saw a friendly face, round, moon-shaped; he knew she had to be native. He felt a kinship with her that relaxed him a little.

He stood smiling at the pretty dark brunette at the information desk. She held out a brown hand, "Rose," she said

"Hi, I'm Sean, you Indian too?" he asked the clerk.

"Yes. Gabrielano," she said. "Full," she added

"Paiute, half,'" said Sean. "I'm the one who called in for the medics, I mean the ambulance, to pick that woman up from the highway. Deputy Vargas must have told you I'd be coming by. I wanted to see her and make sure she was okay. And I wouldn't mind a thank you from her either, you know. We guys love to be heroes. Ex-military," he added.

"Oh, you must mean Erin," Rose said and then covered her mouth. "Whoops, forget I ever said that please. You know we do everything we can to protect the patient's identity. And in her case, we only had a first name. You'll really need to contact Deputy Vargas for more information."

"I know, but I don't like dealing with guys in uniforms; too many years on active duty, it triggers a lot of emotion for me." At this, Sean looked down at his hands, one of them missing part of a finger and one with obvious burns across it.

"Jeez, I know, my brother too. He had a bad accident in a jeep when he was in Iraq; it messed him up. I'm sorry you have troubles still," Rose said. Sean noticed she'd softened her tone of voice.

"Her cousin came. She was nice but very nervous. Blond like her," Rose said. Sometimes this happened to him; people told him things they shouldn't.

A buzzer went off down the hall and the clerk said, "Excuse me, sir, I have to go see what that's about." As she turned to go, he noticed she had left a file on the desk. All it said was "Erin," with a question mark for the last name. He lifted the front cover, in scrawling writing was a name, "Martha Connelly." *That must be her cousin*, Sean thought as he quickly closed the cover, then turned the file around.

There was something about his face, he'd been told, a sort of openness; his expression, interested but poker-faced, led people to spill the beans to him. And sometimes, he got pictures in his head that he didn't totally understand, but his foster mother had told him it was a gift and a curse for him. "Sometimes you might learn things about people you'd rather not," his foster mother had told him.

He waited for Rose to return before leaving. He had managed to coax a name from her. And he had gotten the cousin's name. Sean gave her one last smile, "Bye, and thanks, Rose," he said. She gave him a smile back. He could often count on his looks and his charm to get him what he wanted. "Survival skills," his therapist would say.

He walked out of the hospital and into the warm, dry desert air, stretched, and then unbuckled his helmet from the back of the Q-link. His helmet was a mess, and his bike too. Tatted with dead bugs all over the windshield, the hand guards, and the front fender. Locusts this time of year and butterflies too. Well, he'd wash the bike off a little when he stopped for gas. He carefully folded the plastic ziplock bag that had Erin's pink scarf and like a treasure, hid it down deep into a saddle bag.

"Erin, Irish like me," he said out loud as he swung his leg over the seat and kick-started his reliable old scooter. Erin...he had that much. His brain was whirling with a million questions about the blond Erin.

He saw the sign for his old elementary school, *Tumbleweed,* and decided to swerve and drive by to see how much it might have changed since he went there.

Tumbleweed, a perfect name for his first school, Sean thought as he parked his motorcycle down the block and walked back to look at the playground. Only a few little kids here on a Sunday. Probably kids who lived nearby and wanted to use the swings or that nice newer equipment, slides with happy faces. He didn't remember anything that nice or clean when he went here, but then he didn't remember much. And he only remembered a few things from before *Tumbleweed.*

He cringed involuntarily when he saw himself as a kid, less than six years old, so sad, sitting in the corner with a bowl to catch his tears. When the bowl was full, he was to bring it to his mother and drink the tears from the bowl in front of her. "Boys don't cry!" he'd heard again and again, but somehow he couldn't keep the tears from falling, but they never filled the bowl.

Even if he didn't make a sound, his mother always knew he was still crying. She'd sit brushing her long straight black hair watching him make sure the bowl didn't move from beneath his eyes. It was a hard position to hold as he waited for the tears to slip

34

over the lip of the bowl, small and silver and "the special bowl," as his mom had called it. Each time.

His dad was more direct, at least, when he was home. It was simply "Yes sir" and absolutely no tears, even over a badly skinned knee, or he'd get a belting. Sean shivered that night when he sat in the dog pen with his big dog Tarzana, counting the stars above in the desert sky. The stars had been out for hours, he was sure, because he'd had to start counting over again. He could count to 100. He was sitting in the pen with the dog's head in his lap when the Deputy arrived and shined a flashlight into his face. Tarzana got up and barked and growled and snapped at the Sheriff until the man had to hit him with something, and Tarzana slumped to the ground. Sean remembered yelling at the Deputy. Then a woman came and helped him pack up his few clothes and one or two toys and took him to a place with bright lights that looked like a hospital. He'd seen the inside of quite a few hospitals by then. They all looked the same to him. He didn't know where his mom was, and he was afraid to ask.

The next day the same woman, Debbie, told him all about his new family. It was as if he was just getting born again, with a different mom and dad, sister and brother. He'd never been able to find out what happened to his real baby sister Sandy. He still wondered about her, but it seemed so much trouble to try to look for her at this point. He was in his early 40's now, so she would be about 37 or 38. That was all so long ago. "Maybe it would be better left alone," Jean, his foster mother, had told him when he thought about doing an internet search after he'd come home from Afghanistan. Sandy had been put up for adoption, but his mother "just couldn't let him go," as Debbie and many others quoted her from his files over the years. He had only seen his mother a few times, usually at the Welfare Department office with a social worker there sitting close by. His mother always smelled like the desert, like sage, as he now knew. She didn't ever say much but always left him an arrowhead or a rock.

He walked back and sat on his motorcycle, and took a long swig from his water bottle. He wiped the sweat from his forehead. The school had really loosened a flood for him, one image after another.

For that first week with the Sanchez family, he kept waiting for the sound of a belt whizzing through belt loops and the puff of air as it was being raised for the strike because he was crying, even if it was in his new room at night when there was little danger of anyone hearing him. Still, his foster mother Jean heard him once, and came in to sit with him on his new bed.

"I'll go get the bowl for my tears if you'll tell me where to find it, " Sean whispered to her.

She simply took him in her arms. She rocked him back and forth.

"It's all right to cry. We all do it once in a while, and here, you will not have to collect your tears in a bowl." The loud way she said it had made him shiver.

She'd almost slammed the door shut when she'd left him tucked into his fresh new sheets with owls staring out at him, and he wondered if he had made her mad anyway with his crying. He heard her coughing outside his door, but really, he thought it might be her way of crying. That's how it had been with his real mom. She never cried, but she yelled, and she coughed a lot.

He was very thankful for so many kindnesses the Sanchez family had shown him. His foster father, Paul, was a little gruff but always teaching Sean, always picking him up after school or up from someone's house where he'd gotten into a fistfight. And Abigail, who could make him laugh no matter what. His foster brother, Vincent, was sometimes mean; he liked to tease Sean, but then all kids were like that, weren't they? Sean snapped on his helmet. He was ready to leave the school and the memories behind.

He heard the clank of a basketball hitting a rim, and he thought of his foster father putting up a tether ball in the backyard. Sean spent hours slugging it, making the chain clank against the metal pole over and over again, even when no one was there to

36

play with him. And he and Vincent really went after each other with that tether ball, trying to smash each other with it. And laughing and making farting noises, then laughing even harder.

Sean started his bike. He needed to find a hotel and spend the night tonight. He didn't want to sleep outside again in his tent. Tomorrow he would hike and find a place to hide the scarf. He didn't feel safe with what might be contraband but which he saw as a solid connection.

Chapter 6
Dining in Cole Valley

It took them a few minutes of silence as they recovered from the angry exchange in the park with the panhandler. Najid seemed serious as they slowly walked to the restaurant.

"Elizabeth, why don't you call me *Nej,* like my other American friends do?"

"*Nej*, well, I guess I can get used to that, but I do love saying your full name, Najid." She stressed the "e" sound of his name. "Almost everyone calls me Elizabeth," she said, "but you could give me a nickname..."

"Okay, what about I call you *Betta*?" He looked into her eyes.

They rounded the corner and saw a line in front of the restaurant. She was quiet and then said, "Okay, I think that's fine. You can call me *Betta*. But only you, no one else can." She liked the way it sounded when he said it, "*Betta*", but pronounced like the second letter in the Greek alphabet.

Najid smiled as he gave their names at the door to the host. Nej and Betta. The young man didn't bother asking for spelling, or say he only needed one name; he just scribbled their nicknames down on the list. "Table for two will come quickly," he assured them.

They wanted to sit outside on this rare warm San Francisco evening. They followed the waitress, walking around all the dogs that were allowed on the back patio this particular night.

"I'm glad to come here. Although I'm not a big fan of dogs in cafes, I like all the wood, the vines, and the outdoors. The place feels and smells good. Thank you for picking this for us," Najid said. "Why don't we share the starter of Mediterranean roasted vegetables and get some beers?"

When a tall young waiter brought the beer and placed the appetizer in the middle of the table, Elizabeth felt happy.

"What else can I get for you tonight?" the waiter asked, with a slight accent; maybe French, maybe Portuguese. Elizabeth couldn't really decide.

Najid ordered a Moroccan lamb tagine, and she asked for the salmon in a pesto crust.

After they had ordered, a speckled puppy, furry, maybe an Australian Shepherd, came over to lick their feet. The owner pulled the young dog back and said, "Sorry, he loves shoes."

Elizabeth looked at Najid, and he started to laugh and then she started laughing too. Najid lifted his beer and clicked glasses.

"To Betta."

"To Nej," she added. They smiled, and he took an extra long swig of his dark brew.

When the beautifully plated main dishes arrived looking delicious, Elizabeth was longing for the taste of lamb. "That looks so good, Najid," she said.

"Nej," he reminded her. "Have some, Betta," he said, holding out a bite for her.

"Oh, I don't eat lamb anymore," she said, even though her hand was reaching for the fork. She took the bite off the fork and handed it back. "Delicious," she said.

They had finished their beer, and now Najid was waving in the direction of the waiter. "We need to order wine," he said and looked at her. "You'll have one, won't you? Instead of another beer."

She nodded yes. "We would like a bottle of sauvignon blanc and two wine glasses," Najid said to the waiter.

"Just pick a good one for us," Najid added.

So far, she thought, *except for the incident with the panhandler, this evening is off to a great start.* She felt happy and warmed and so thankful to be with this man sipping her wine and devouring her dinner. Perhaps later, there would be something more, but for now, this was perfect.

"I lived in Pakistan for four years, and I was very interested in everything Persian, but books on Zoroaster especially, were hard to find. I had to look in some little back alley shops for books," Elizabeth said, remembering their conversation that first night in The Jewel of India.

"I know; my Persian grandmother must be one of the last of our family to know all about it," Najid said. "And she wanted me to be named Ahuramazda, but my mother gave me a Muslim name. In spite of that, Grandmother always called me Ahura."

"What does it mean?" Elizabeth asked.

"It is lord, or wise god, something like that," he said smiling.

As an Asian History major, Elizabeth loved the details but hated the outcomes. Even the Persian leader, Nadir Shah, came from a family of herdsmen to became a Persian boy warrior, turning out to be just another empire builder—*another in a long line of tyrants,* Elizabeth thought. "It seems to me that one man's sacred is another's burden or banishment."

Najid looked at her until finally she explained,

"Oh excuse me, Najid, I mean Nej, I was just upset all over again because of the recent terrorist attacks. Why does it always come down to a contest of the gods and which is the true God."

"I know, I know. The world's always in a mess, Betta," he answered, suddenly looking very sad, a frown across his forehead.

They had a slow walk home; there was still plenty of light. This time they avoided the park. As they were walking. he held her hand, and then he suddenly stopped and reached over to pull her close to him. He kissed her, first on the cheek, but then they both shared a surprisingly passionate kiss.

"Pheew," Elizabeth said, "We could have lit up a small city with that one." She didn't mean to say anything; she had intended to just savor the moment quietly, but she just had to. Najid laughed and kissed her again. His kisses were warm and sensual.

That night they left a pile of clothes by the front door and ended up on her white silk cover. Things progressed quickly, so

40

quickly she forgot to give him a condom from out of her bedside table. And he remembered that detail a little too late. Neither wanted this lovemaking to stop. They seemed like animals who'd been deprived of food, hungry for it.

She always preferred to sleep by herself, never had been one for spooning, and it seemed awkward now that the peak had come and gone. After holding each other for about 20 minutes, she finally had to tell him he wouldn't be spending the night with her in her bed.

"That's fine, I understand. But, I hope someday you will accept me into your bed for the night."

She watched Najid pick up his clothes, admiring his body, lean but muscular and with curly black hair on his chest. He smiled at her in the darkened room, his teeth gleaming. It was not unlike a wolf that had just satisfied his mate and himself, like that photograph she had seen one time in Palm Springs.

He was handsome everywhere, and she had just gone with passion. He pulled on his pants, then carefully buttoned his shirt. Then tugged on his shoes without the socks.

While he tied his shoelaces, she climbed under the covers, and he came over to sit for a minute. He didn't have anything to say for a change. He just kissed her cheek and patted her face. Then, pulling the front door closed, he left. After a few minutes, she opened the door, looked out into the dark, all the street lights on, shut the door again, shut the deadbolt, and this time pulled the chain across. *City life,* she thought.

Long after he had gone, in the middle of the night, she was a little cold. She got up and cleaned up and then slipped on pajamas. While she was brushing her teeth, she saw herself in the mirror, a happy mess, with hair flying out in all directions.

Chapter 7
Petroglyphs

Sean needed a real place to spend the night, wash up and collect himself. He needed to decide whether to stay a few days or even longer to try to trace the woman. Sometimes he would get a picture in his mind to show him where something or someone was, and he was hoping that by staying in the area, something would come to him. It was a strange gift he'd had for as long as he could remember. He simply accepted it as normal, even if others didn't.

He looked around his motel room, it's lack of color, in a sandy place, the surrounding hills a pale purple. The town was a mess that looked like every other sprawling suburb near Los Angeles—except maybe with the poverty more obvious. *Well, it'll do*, he thought as he set his pack down on the twin bed and headed to the shower. He had grabbed a quick burger in town, and the sun, the food, and the day with its rough memories had worn him out. He was asleep as soon as he pulled up the covers.

The next morning he brewed coffee in his room and drank it. Sean thought the coffee wasn't very good, but at least he'd made it strong. He ate an energy bar, tucking a few more alongside an apple into the small backpack where his water bottle was firmly attached. He also packed a compass and his camera. He leaned against the wall as he laced up his hiking boots and headed out into the hot morning air. There was no traffic, but still, the distant click and whir of fans slicing through the desert air created a whole new landscape. Harnessing the desert winds for power, wind farms dotted the hills.

He put the pink scarf in a small cardboard box and tossed it into his backpack. He thought that the best way to protect it was to bury it until he could find the woman, the blond. He started his bike and took off.

He rode about 20 minutes to the Vasquez Rocks. He locked his bike and started walking on a path well-marked with boulders here and there, with a mix of shrubs and desert vegetation sprouting up, even through the cracks in the rocks. The place was mostly rock outcrops, slanted and spiky and magnificent. There were the occasional skittering lizards, but so far, no rattlers and no coyotes to be seen. He hiked until he reached a spring—a giant pool of water underneath this dry sandy soil. It seemed such a contradiction he'd never gotten used to... the palms appearing out of dry hills, mist spraying up over the rocks. Up ahead would be a creek leading to a waterfall.

He sat down and took the map out of his pack. He'd circled all the places that were special to him as a kid, the places he'd go to straighten out his head and calm down. He was sitting in one of those places now, and there were his initials chiseled into a log over the creek just below the waterfall. Now, he knew better than to leave behind any evidence of his hike, but when he was a boy, he clamored for people to know he existed—that he had been to these places. He traced the rough letters *SQ* with his thumb and couldn't help smiling. It was still here: evidence he'd been a kid and he'd been here. Vasquez Rocks offered experienced hikers a good workout, and if you just kept going, you'd reach the Pacific Crest Trail, a place he'd always wanted to walk. Maybe someday he'd do it.

He kept going until he saw the rock with the petroglyphs. Spirals and images that looked like a shining sun, some faces, and a few rudimentary animals in red. He turned off the trail and looked for a good spot to dig a hole for the box with the scarf. He had just finished covering it with sand and sticks when he heard a couple of voices, hikers heading toward the waterfall. He took a long cool drink of water and then hooked his water jug back onto his backpack. He decided to go back down the rocky path toward town. But then he remembered his camera and took a few pictures, some of the rocks, and one of the spot where the scarf lay hidden.

"Howdy," he said as he approached the hikers. It was a couple of young women who looked like they hiked a lot. They had on all the right equipment and were attacking the trail with solid speed. They had a goal in mind and after seeing the movie, Wild, he realized they probably were training for that long, grueling hike: the Pacific Crest Trail.

"Hi," said the short one with her long hair worn back in a ponytail.

"How far to the waterfall?" asked the girl with very short black hair.

"Almost there," Sean answered over his shoulder. The blond woman reminded him again of Erin. He felt nervous; he hoped nobody would find the scarf. There were still the occasional treasure hunters in these hills, looking for silver bricks or other contraband rumored to be hidden in these steep boulder-laden hills by Vasquez and his gang. Ah, he felt a sense of freedom and release, just doing nothing but concentrating on putting one foot in front of the other, heading down.

When he got to his motorbike, he threw his leg over and started the engine. He'd pack up his things and get going toward the coast first thing in the morning. But, just as he rounded a bend before the motel, a picture came into his head, the way his mind worked sometimes. The woman Erin—he saw her with a man in a military uniform.

"Air Force!" he shouted out into the desert.

After grabbing a quick bite to eat at a diner, he headed back to his motel. It was still hot when he'd finished drinking a bubbly cola. He left out the clothes he would wear for his trip home. And took a long shower, pulling out a pair of boxer shorts to sleep in. He checked his emails on his funky smartphone, which barely had any storage left on it, and then sank under the light covers. He reached over for his notebook and scribbled a quick reminder to call his surf buddies to check in before he left. He was already two days late for a meet-up in San Diego. *But then again, they probably knew better than to actually expect him to show up when he said he would,* he thought to himself, grinning.

In the middle of the night, when he had tossed off the motel covers and was thrashing around, he remembered the dream that woke him.

He was holding a jewel-encrusted box, and when he opened it, a rabbit was sleeping in it. Startled, the rabbit leaped up and started hopping around him. And then the rabbit turned pink and then red and slowly became a red rose growing from the floor to the ceiling.

It seemed a pleasant, if puzzling, dream—but then he remembered some words. "Rose, deep red, drop of blood, finger prick rose metal, formed, unyielding beauty. Rabbit, soft brown striated. Scared, wants out. Box, carved, roses and rabbits, bright villages, ancient horizons, secrets, alive and holding all that is needed."

These dreams and words were always a puzzle to be pieced together over days, months and years. His foster mother, Jean, had taught him how to hang on to the images and words and write them down in a little notebook. He dug into his packed duffel until he pulled out a ragged book and quickly wrote down what he could remember of the dream and the most important words.

He saw the dream as filled with good omens. The words he had written meant that since the box he had hidden had the pink scarf, paisleys, and that woman, Erin, she had a rose tattoo.

"Ancient horizons, secrets, alive, holding all that is needed," he said out loud as he walked to the office to settle his bill.

"Hasta la vista, baby," he yelled out as he rode off on his motorbike. He waved goodbye to no one in particular, to Palmdale, the desert, to the seedy motel. He left behind bad old memories and a few good ones. He was on his way to water and waves and friends and Corona beers, trading the hot, dry air for the cool, foggy shores. He swung back and forth like the metronome ticking on the top of the piano back when his sister was still taking her lessons.

46

At least he'd hidden the scarf in a safe spot to collect when he was ready for it.

He felt liberated as his little motorcycle broke the quiet morning, adding its tinny engine sounds to the sound, fainter now, of the wind turbines and the airport. The wind was starting to pick up and blow the tumbleweeds across the highway.

He could hardly wait for that first glimpse of the ocean.

Chapter 8
The Color Red and Poets

Elizabeth had only heard from Najid once since the second night they slept together. They'd spent the day hiking and then picked up pizza and brought it to her place. Before they even opened the pizza box, they'd had all their clothes off and were happily making love. At least they'd used a condom; he had brought one with him and took it out as they fell into her bed. He was whispering into her ear in what she knew was Persian Farsi. They had fantastic sex, and their bodies matched so well—both tall and lean, with muscular legs and arms. They could cling well to each other, and either one could be on top.

Afterward, he got up, and when he came back from the bathroom, he had her bathrobe in his hand. He pulled his briefs on and said, "Come on, let's eat. I'm starved."

This night they finished the entire large pizza. But when he took her hand and started to head back to the bedroom again, she asked him to leave, and he did so willingly. He nodded; he understood now that this might be the routine. He could be her lover, but not share her bed all night. She was glad she didn't have to say again that it made her uncomfortable to have him there the whole night and for them to wake up together in the morning.

He'd called a few days later to thank her for the evening and say that he was off again on a business trip. Disappointing but not unexpected.

She had been marking off the calendar, old fashioned way, to track this relationship, as well as her monthly cycle on her phone app. Her period was a week late. She was worried—that first night when they didn't use anything, they'd just shed their clothes and made mad love without thinking of anything else.

"I won't be able to call for a while," he had said. "I'll be in the Middle East and then India. But I'll get in touch as soon as I return, I promise."

"Damn it," she said for what must have been the tenth time. Maybe he was just going to be one of those pretty men who slept with as many women as possible and kept women as handy sex toys, nothing much more. He probably never planned on settling down, at least not now.

Bah. She didn't place much trust in anything or anyone when it came to relationships.

She'd only been in love twice before—once ended in marriage, and then the marriage ended as her young husband took less and less interest in her, in spending time together, or in having sex with her. He started to verbally pick at her until it became a daily routine. Finally she erupted in tears and he in shouts. They both agreed it was time to get a divorce. It was only later that she found he'd begun to sleep with men and women after meet-ups of groups practicing Tantric sex. He'd never even asked her if she might be interested in their own one-on-one Tantric sex.

Her second love had been ViJay. Toward the end of their five-year affair, Elizabeth suspected he might be starting to see her sister. But that wasn't important because he'd decided he couldn't stay and planned to return to India. Her sister Deirdre had always done pretty much as she pleased, and she had seen her and ViJay together once.

She'd asked her, "You and ViJay seem a little too close, Deirdre. What is going on?"

"Do you really care sister? You said you were done with him."

She had said it, but had Elizabeth really meant it? It was more like ViJay was through with her, and she could feel it coming; he was about to leave her. He had told her he was going back home.

She planned to visit him a year later, but he'd said an emphatic, "NO! to that." No explanations. *But of course*, she thought, *he'd be moving on to someone else.*

She couldn't even maintain good contact with her sister, even though she had tried. And now her cousin, Martha, left a message saying that Deirdre had been in a hospital but was basically okay. Then nothing more, and she hadn't been able to find out where, or any of the details. When she re-dialed the phone number left on her cell phone, it was some donut place in the desert. And her cousin's phone number was disconnected. Still, she felt guilty for not following up, for not making sure her sister was really okay. Most people would be on it, but then, they didn't have a sister like Deirdre, who seemed to never need much from anybody else.

Elizabeth was going to go for a bike ride today. She wasn't sure she had enough energy for a full bike ride. She would just head out toward the Golden Gate and keep going until she was tired. But today, fatigue pulled her down, even though it was only mid-morning.

As she took off her white terry cloth robe, she noticed a spot of red. Ah, she was safe—though she wasn't sure if she was relieved or disappointed. Her feelings lately had been a broiling brew of contradictions and angst. Cramps made her think about changing her plans to go for a bouncy ride, but she decided to go anyway. Modern woman and all—though not modern enough to think about offering Najid a condom. But her period had come, and everything was okay, wasn't it?

She headed out through the back streets and alleyways. She rode to the Marin side of the Golden Gate bridge and then turned around, walking her bike. She stopped and looked over the railing. Small dots of sailboats were taking full advantage of the winds which were pushing the fog back to the ocean. She could understand why people picked this spot to jump. The idea of flying, of this scene being the last beauty you would ever see in this lifetime.

The air was so clean and fresh today. Soon she was riding again and feeling much better. All it took was a little bit of grandeur to improve her spirits. She focused on pedaling, and the bridge, the bay, and how this view of the entrance to the Pacific couldn't be beat. Suddenly she noticed that her cramps had increased and she stopped to rub her belly. She searched around in her backpack until she found an Advil. Oh, the familiar pain of womanhood. Call it enough for today.

But what if her period had not come? What would she have done? Would she have told Najid, and what would his reaction have been? Oh well, she didn't need to think about that any longer.

Her cell phone ticked as she wheeled her bike into the backyard. A message, a picture, nothing more—a paisley scarf just like the one she had, except it was a deep red. The phone number was nothing she recognized, just paisleys aflame against a black background. Where was the text message? Maybe it was someone from her graduate school program. They all knew fabric was her fascination.

Or could it be Najid? If so, it was a funny way to communicate something. What was the message? He was thinking of her? This morning she had no patience for puzzles or cuteness, her belly aching with the start of menstruation. And soon her birthday was coming, a big one at that: she'd be 40, and nothing settled yet in her life. School still hanging, no real boyfriend, no family. She felt weighed down by these thoughts. On the weekend, a few friends were going to take her out to dinner, and then they would go clubbing. Bring in the next decade with her.

The next morning, her flow slowed down until it was just spots. Normally, at this point, her period it would be strong with a few more days to go. Ah sweet mysteries of the female body. Hormones. And she had heard that what lay ahead—flashing heat, mood swings—was no better.

Well, at least today, she'd feel back to normal and able to pursue the question of who and why the picture of the scarf came. Not pink, like hers, but a full deep red. Not so much soft, but a more dynamic and regal color. She wheeled her bike around to the back and secured the lock on the wheels.

Suddenly, there was a loud knock at the door. When she opened it, she couldn't help herself from saying in almost a whisper, "Hey, stranger, it's you."

Without even calling first, there he was at her door. Najid had taken a cab from the airport.

"Oh, Najid, just give me a minute, alright?" She went into the bathroom, cleaned up and put on a pair of jeans, the looser ones, and a sweatshirt. She returned to the kitchen and Najid.

He reached out to hand her something, but instead took her into his arms and give her a tight hug followed by a big kiss right on the lips. Just a sweet, plump, lips-to-lips kiss. For a minute, she felt elated and confused all at the same time. What in the world was going on with her and this man, a near stranger?

"Here, and please, don't call me a stranger," he said handing her an elaborately wrapped box. "Something I brought from my travels, something I think you will like."

Beware, she thought, *remember those spiders who offer a package wrapped in their own silk in order to get the female to mate with them.* But what the hell; she had already mated, and quite successfully. Her face flushed red. Thankfully he could not read her thoughts.

"What is it? Are you just so surprised?" he asked, smiling at her. "I remember; your birthday is now."

He'd heard her tell him when they were hiking and remembered. Well, now; how in the world could she explain that she had felt deserted? That she had longed for him and even thought she might have had his baby growing inside? No, she said nothing, but quietly took the gift setting it down on the table.

"Can I make you some coffee?" she asked, reaching for the can of Peet's Arabian Mocha Java.

"Only if it's black and nothing sweet," he added. "Aren't you going to open it?" he asked, pointing to the package. She looked at him and smiled.

"Yes, I can hardly imagine what it might be," she said, undoing the big bow and opening the box.

"Card first," he insisted.

She picked up the card, placed it on the top of layers of tissue, and started to quietly read the message.

"Aloud please," Najid said with a big smile on his face.

"At night, I open the window and ask the moon to come and press its face against mine.

Breathe into me. Close the language-door and open the love-window. The moon won't

use the door, only the window". ~ Rumi."

"Najid, that is so beautiful, so, well, I can't even say how it makes me feel." Elizabeth was at a loss for words. She forgot all about making the coffee and just pushed him lightly onto a chair and then sat on his lap. She kissed him, his eyelids, his cheeks, his nose, his mouth.

"Okay, now finish. You didn't even see the presents," Najid said still holding her on his lap.

Elizabeth turned back layers of tissue to uncover a small book wrapped in a red scarf, the scarf she had seen in the text message. Mystery solved. She read the title of the book: *The Persian Poets*. "Shouldn't this be bigger and fatter? There are so many Persian poets and even Neruda, with his translated poems." she said.

Najid just laughed and played with the curls of her hair.

"Can we make love now?" Najid looked at her

"Is that what the gifts were for?" she asked.

"No, the gifts were to show I missed you and well, I like you very very much." Najid said very seriously, gazing into her eyes.

"Najid, it's not a good time for me... it's that time of the month." For a minute he looked blank and then he got it. "Okay," he said giving her a hug. "Let's just talk and hug, and can I at least kiss you?"

"I've missed you Najid. I turn forty on Friday."

"Forty is good. I know, I've been in the forties now for awhile! Soon I will cook a Persian dinner for you, at my place to celebrate. but maybe tomorrow we can hike again, I want to see more of this San Francisco. I heard there are parrots and we should go find them."

She was still thinking about what he said, that he was eventually going to cook a Persian dinner for her. She felt so overwhelmed that all she could do was put the book down and kiss him again. She was feeling so tired and shocked by his sudden appearance and all the attention after his long absence she just stood there saying nothing. She just looked at him. She was attracted to him, and wanted to go to bed with him, but she still felt a bit of queasiness that just wouldn't stop.

Soon, an invitation to his place. She didn't even know where he lived. Somehow they were reaching a different level, close enough that he would cook for her.

It all sounded good, but of course right now she didn't have much of an appetite. Maybe she'd picked up a parasite somewhere in India and just now it was making itself known. All she knew was this tiredness, this bug—whatever it was—would finally go away, and she would get her appetite for everything back again. At least she knew it wasn't Covid, she'd just tested a few days ago, and anyway, thankfully the virus was dying back now.

They moved to her little loveseat, and he told her about the book, about his favorite poets. And he said he had bought the scarf because he knew how much she loved her pink paisley scarf.

She thought to herself, then, she had accepted the gifts from the spider. She was opening the love window, despite her better instincts.

Chapter 9
Internet Search

Sean drove over the foothills toward San Diego and then up the coast to Oceanside. He parked his motorcycle near his front door. His place smelled a little musty, but the air coming in the window was refreshingly moist after the dry desert heat. He opened all the windows and left his door open.

The next-door neighbor, Trevor, waved, a joint hanging off his fingers. *Surfers sure love their pot,* Sean thought.

He didn't.

Trevor, a guy in his 50s, always said he supported the military, but had never picked up a big automatic rifle in his life, never had heard the sound of one ringing in his ears. He didn't know what war zones really meant to the soldiers, let alone the people unfortunate to be living in one. Trevor was the guy who fed his cat whenever Sean was gone. A feral cat who had decided Sean could be counted on for food and an ear scratch. Trevor also let Sean cobble off his internet connection. So, in important ways, Trevor was a good neighbor.

What did Sean really know about the blond woman from the desert? He thought back to the person he'd found on the side of the road. Not moving. Appeared to be in her 30's but could be older. She was pale, on the tall side but with a rather slight build. Long hair. Tattoo...roses. Pink scarf. But what else? Sean closed his eyes and held his head in his hands waiting for an image to come to him.

He saw her bent over her computer, in drab colored clothes, pants and a tan, long-sleeved T-shirt, and she seemed like she was hiding, hunkered down in a room that had very few lights. *She's scared,* he thought, *and she's hiding out.* And then a flash and the next sight he had was of her being driven down a small highway, sand dunes on either side, on the seat, her legs folded up under her in a yoga position. Lotus. Her hair was black, not blond.

She's so afraid that she left the hospital before she really recovered. That's what his intuition was telling him. She'd been left for dead, and so it made sense that she did not want to be found.

Someone was hunting her.

Right after he found her, he had a flash of her next to a man in a uniform, Air Force. In his vision, she was standing in the dark, and she had a hospital gown on. He didn't know much, but he had her name now, and that was worth a lot. That would take him down the dark tunnel of the internet, where he was sure to find her.

Erin Connelly... same last name as her cousin, maybe? And maybe Irish, like half of him. He would play the Irish card this time, not the Native card. That is, if he could get in touch with her. If he could get a solid lead off his computer, his funky older laptop.

That pink scarf, like so many he'd seen in booths in Pakistan... hanging in rows, or the shawls neatly folded into like-colored stacks of pashminas. Hers had to have come from there. Maybe a boyfriend in the military? Maybe even someone at Edwards Air Force Base? The base wasn't too far from where she was dumped. And he assumed she was dumped.

Sean did a few stretches, changed into his sweats and sat down on the one good chair he had in front of his rescued Formica kitchen table. He opened Google; today's Google banner celebrating the birthday of a woman scientist, but he didn't have time to check it out as he usually did. He needed to get to work. He was still worried that Erin was in some kind of deep danger, and he felt compelled to help her.

He took a few deep yoga breaths in and out and said to nobody but himself, "Let me find her and may she be well." Affirmations....he'd been raised on them.

He typed in her name from the file he'd seen in the hospital: "Erin" and then with her cousin's last name, "Connelly." It turned out to be a common Irish name, but he did see a listing for an "Ethnobotanist" based in the Los Angeles area. He clicked on that name, and it listed a number for a woman in Long Beach who was

42. Her relatives: Teo Carrizo and Arguello Carrizo. Jeez, he wondered, could this be the pale Erin of the desert? He typed in Teo Carrizo and there was a YouTube video of a kid, about 9 years old, dancing, Latin, with rhythm. It was under Mateo Carrizo's name. He re-entered Erin's name as Erin Connelly Carrizo, and that led him to several Carrizos—and one Erin C. Carrizo.

"Bingo," Sean said out loud. He tried her name both ways, Carrizo Connelly and Connelly Carrizo.

Erin (Carrizo) Connelly, Ethnobotonist.

The website had her picture.

He stopped and took a deep breath. Her face was fuller, the hair blond but shorter, and she looked on top of the world. Proud, happy and smart. In one picture, she had a white lab coat on and held a plant, the kind that grows off trees, with multiple air roots. Something from South America or Indonesia, probably. Under the picture, it identified the plant as a 'Tillandsia'. He waited for the intense feeling of pain in his ribs to subside. *I haven't felt that injury for years*, he thought. Six ribs broken in Afghanistan. He knew this was strong. This was his Erin. His body was a reliable truth detector, better than any machine.

Sean read through a list of titles of all the papers Erin had published. There was a link to "Plant Universe with the 'Plant Woman', and on her Plant Woman page, she just used the name Dr. C: Plant Woman.

Plant Woman.

Hm. Now what?

When he clicked on the contact button, it said: *This information is no longer available.* Dead end. But now he knew she was an ethnobotanist, and she lived in Southern California, maybe not far from where he lived. But she seemed very much in hiding. Removed contact information from her website.

Plants… someone had told him that the military was always searching for plants as weapons or cures. He'd heard that mustard gas had been based on volatile mustard oils and synthesized into the dreaded weapon. But then his foster mother had made mustard plasters for him when he'd come home sore from a too-long hike. And sometimes, when he got bronchitis, or bad asthma that wouldn't let up, she would gently rub it in and wrap it with cheesecloth, winding it around his chest. She always told him, "Plants are powerful."

Sean had the husband's name, Mateo, and probably a son, Arguello. Now he'd really have to dig in. This was getting more and more interesting for him. He had a big grudge against anything the military did. He was completely disillusioned after his time in the service, and now, it looked like a build-up to the next hot spot—back to Korea again, or even Iran. Maybe even Russia or China. Already in Ukraine. He guessed warfare would just never end. Too much money to be made from oil sucked from the earth, from making and selling weapons, or just the need for men to dominate.

To prove whose dick was really the longest, he thought, chuckling softly at the ironies of life.

He clicked off his laptop, went into the bedroom to take off his sweats, and pulled on his swim trunks. He rubbed his leg— shrapnel scars. He squeezed some white zinc out of its tube and applied it over his nose and cheeks and then picked up the sunscreen and sprayed the rest of his face, his arms and over his scars. There was nothing quite like the stinging of a scar when it's sunburned, except for maybe stinging nettles when you accidentally stepped on them bare-footed in the foothills near Palmdale.

The waves sounded like they were holding up just fine, with a bit of an off-shore breeze to ensure that they did. He grabbed his shortboard and began the walk to the ocean. His home away from home, both places filled with shimmering; the desert waves, heat-induced mirages of water; the ocean, the sun flicking off the water, almost blinding sometimes. The desert with pools of hidden water underneath; the ocean with life teaming below. His homes were so alike, and yet, so very different. The California off-shore winds were great for the surfers, but bound to start a fire in the autumn.

Sean thought that after a morning of good rides, he might just stop by the Tidal Wave for coffee and doughnut holes. The Tidal Wave was a surfer hang-out where a very cute waitress served up the cups of coffee and brought out big trays of generously-portioned breakfasts. He had a major crush on MaeAnn, who had come over from Hawaii. She had long dark hair, almost always pinned up with a pair of big wooden combs. He had imagined her hair many times, flowing down her back, as he held her close. But thanking her and giving her a smile was about as close as he'd come to her so far. Maybe this time, without his laptop, which was a convenient way to stay awhile, he might make more of a connection. He might even ask her where in Hawaii she was from, or something—anything small to start a conversation.

Sean mused about the internet and how it was relatively easy to find anyone and anything. He hadn't grown up with computers; he was in his late forties now. Still, like everyone else, he counted on his phone and his laptop for important news and sometimes completely unimportant emails.

After coffee, he would go back home and resume his search. He would try finding Theo Carrizo to get to the Plant Woman and ensure she was safe. And later, he would come out as a heroic human being, not just some former military guy getting by on the occasional photo sale, and disability pay from the army, but as a true man. A man who could save a woman and maybe, with any luck, soon date a woman—MaeAnn. He waited, watching for a good set. Finally he saw a swell forming that he looked good, and he started to paddle hard. He took off on a wave and felt the edge of his board catch, the water pulling him over the crest and down into a great little ride.

Chapter 10
Pink

These kits were reliable. Two pink lines meant you're pregnant. There was no doubt about it.

She'd been waiting for this moment for years, wanting it, an urgent desire, just like when you've had good sex with someone for the first time, all you could think of was having sex again, even when you were supposed to be writing a thesis.

"Wow, I'm actually pregnant!" Elizabeth yelled out loud in her flat. She'd bought the test kit earlier in the day and waited until bedtime. It had taken a lot of courage for her to actually unwrap the test stick and read the directions. Then she set the stick down and waited even longer. While she was eager to know and hoped at first that it would confirm what she suspected, she was scared; she was as frightened by the thought of being pregnant as much as she was hoping for it. Her feelings were so mixed up that she just didn't know what to think. It was almost beyond thinking. She'd had a gut reaction. What was that blood last month about if she was really pregnant the whole time? Of course she was very tired and feeling like she would throw up at any minute.

She felt a strong feeling of aversion to the idea of something growing inside of her, taking over the space that had been empty for forty years. There were no sweet images in her head of a small pink baby nuzzling against her breasts, but more like a feeling of being trapped. An image of the house finch at her friend Mindy's, sitting in its metal cage. The bird was so tiny and colorful but with clipped wings. She never considered the finch's songs to be 'cheerful' as Mindy described them, but more mournful and filled with loneliness.

"You need to get Phoebe a mate," she'd said to Mindy. But Mindy never seemed to find the time to pick up a second house finch.

What was wrong with her? Elizabeth had always considered herself to have motherly feelings, and when she'd held her friends' babies, and there'd been more and more of them lately, she felt a kind of special kinship to the baby. What she thought a mother might feel. But now that she was growing one of her own. she was wailing and shouting to no one in particular, "I can't be anyone's mother!"

When she finally stopped sobbing, she went into the kitchen and swung open the refrigerator door to take out a small container of milk. Saltine crackers were lying all over the counter. They had been her main meal for days. Her head was spinning, and her tummy was unsettled. She was so tired, she had to go sit down in her one comfortable chair, the over-sized one with tons of pillows. She propped herself up admiring the texture of the woven wool pillow. How many hours did this take some woman to weave? Or some child worker. *Child... oh,* she thought, *I'm acting so crazy.* And she was sweating right now, beads dripping down her face, her arms. Sweating had been her theme song every night for three weeks. She slowly drank the milk and ate another couple of crackers. *Hormones; they rule the whole world,* Elizabeth thought as she set down her glass and went for a washcloth. She ran it under the water and dabbed the cool cloth across her forehead and under her breasts, which felt achy.

Now, she reminded herself, there was the little problem of telling Najid. He claimed he'd be okay with a baby when she just happened to mention that she wanted one on a date a few weeks ago. They had come back to her place and were in her bed, so that was still just bed talk, words, not real, like these two pink stripes.

Well, she said to herself, "I'd better just get it over with and call him." Abortion would be the sensible thing, but then she never had been sensible. "A baby, I just can't believe it." She held onto the plastic test stick with its two very positive pink stripes like it was a sacred object, gently placing it up on her dresser next to the picture of her grandmother, the one where her grandmother is

61

laughing and dressed in a shiny satin dress, blue with a white collar. Hand-tinted, the photo was taken in a club in the 1940s.

"It was a very special night, the evening your grandfather popped the question."

"What question?"

"Will you be my bride?" She would make her grandmother tell her that story over and over again.

It was getting late, and Elizabeth wondered if Najid would still be awake. She knew he'd said he had a big business meeting in the morning. She got out her cell phone and clicked on his number. After the third ring, she hung up. She walked into the kitchen, the tiles pleasantly smooth against her bare feet. She poured a glass of water into which she tossed fresh mint she'd picked earlier from her tiny kitchen garden. She pressed the glass against her cheeks to soothe herself, and take off some of the heat.

Then suddenly she was shivering with cold. She went into the bedroom, climbed into her all-white bed, and pulled the feather comforter up. The last thing she thought about was the color pink.

Maybe a girl?

******

She was sitting in her grandmother's lap. The feel of satin against her chubby legs was so smooth, almost like glass. Suddenly her grandmother started to move, and soon the glassy feel turned sharp and prickly and then soft. She looked down to see her fat little arm covered in feathers. She looked up, and her grandmother had transformed into a white crane, long neck pointing upward.

Elizabeth was flying next to her grandmother, soaring above a town that was having a carnival, or was it a street filled with stalls and colorful flags flying? She swooped down and tried to land on an oriental rug, droplet patterns in grays, pearl whites and peaches and blue, a very deep blue border as blue as her grandmother's satin dress. But her claws would not really touch down; she could not land. Suddenly she lifted off again. She looked behind her and saw that she was trailing a long tail of purple, green, gold and scarlet feathers. She had never seen anything so

62

beautiful. But, as she flapped her wings to skirt around a tall candlestick, she felt one of her wings catch fire. Both wings were smoking and then on fire. She sailed higher and higher, flames consuming her. Still, she didn't feel anything but slightly hot. She was a phoenix now, aflame in the sky. Still able to fly, she blazed through the dark like a meteorite.

******

She woke up, kicked off the covers and sat up in bed panting. She didn't know what to think. Was that dream a nightmare or a warning? The image of a phoenix was so familiar to her. In Persia, known as Samug, almost every Asian country had a version of this mythical bird.

Death and rebirth.

Birth.

Oh my god, she thought. *Birth.*

Chapter 11
Plans

At the coffee shop that morning, Sean finally had the courage to begin a real conversation with MaeAnn. Then he surprised himself. He heard himself inviting her out for dinner. He was proposing a date.

He had asked very simply, "MaeAnn, I wonder if you would consider having dinner with me? My treat," he added. It felt slightly awkward, but her big smile and a vigorous positive nod of her head gave him the courage to say more.

"Okay, what about that Thai restaurant a couple of blocks over."

"I love Thai food, Sean. I'd be very happy to join you for dinner there. What about this Friday? I get off work early that day, so that would give me time to walk my dog beforehand too."

"Sounds perfect, MaeAnn."

He quickly finished his coffee as MaeAnn went to take orders from new customers. Since he couldn't think of anything more to say, he just left money to pay his bill and walked to the door, waving to MaeAnn as he headed out the door. He would take a long walk and then do a little more surfing to help him relax.

It had been months since he'd actually had a real date that was planned ahead of time, so her acceptance of a dinner date made him happy, but jittery as well. Now he'd have to work on letting go of any negative thinking that might make him back out. He was an essentially shy person and it was hard for him to just chat. He could talk forever on certain subjects. He could discuss anything having to do with the ocean and marine life. He also liked to talk about photography and the solar system. And how the American Indians had been screwed over...but mostly, people didn't want to hear about that. Otherwise, he was lost. He didn't read a lot, mostly small books with few pages, ones that were recommended to him by friends. He did read surfing magazines, free ones he'd pick up

64

at the post office. He didn't read the newspaper. It always put him in a foul mood, so he had given it up shortly after he'd come home still recovering from wounds of all kinds.

Sean was getting ready for bed, and as he always did when he brushed his teeth, he reviewed his day. He'd learned to do this to help him remember things. He put his toothbrush back and walked over to his bed, a simple full sized bed that fit into his tiny place. He pulled back his cotton sheets and the lightweight quilt, made for him by his foster mother, and hoped for a dream that would point him to Erin, the woman with the rose tattoo and the pink scarf. Now that he knew more about her, that she traveled a lot and was known for her expertise in plants that grew in remote areas of the world, it made more sense that she quickly recovered from a coma-like state. She was probably stronger than she looked. She was used to going through jungles, dealing with snakes, using machetes, and fording waterways.

Those marks on her wrists—infusion or sedation through the veins—were clearly meant to not show that much and to quickly disappear. He had constantly inserted lines when he worked as a medic in combat, but usually, it was into an easy-to-find vein near the inside of an elbow. Soldiers were bleeding like crazy, and the veins were not always easy to poke. Everything in combat was in crisis mode, and medical treatment tended to be a little sloppy because saving a life was a real challenge when someone had been blown up. He'd had to develop a tough skin for what he saw, and even then, sometimes at night, he would cry softly in his bunk, hoping no one would hear him.

Everything he'd experienced in combat had made him appreciate where he lived, California, on the coast, in a still affordable, though funky apartment. As he settled down into bed, he tried to put all thoughts of needles and wounds out of his mind. Instead, he said his nightly affirmation, his version of a prayer. "Guide me into the light. Let me be of service. Let me love and be loved. Amen." And then he turned off the table lamp, something bamboo he'd picked up at the local Goodwill. His phone was next to him on the table, just in case it should ring. He felt the drag and pull of sleep, tidal and welcome. In his dreams, he was in the water, and the waves were filled with flowers. A woman who looked like MaeAnn was walking out of the water toward him.

The phone on his bedside table was blinking when he woke up, a message. His sleep was so deep he hadn't even heard the sound of messaging.

His foster sister Abagail had texted: *"I miss you, and I haven't seen you in person for over two years, Sean! I want to celebrate your birthday with you. I know it's a big one, 50, or jeez. maybe only 49? We can watch the sailboat races in the bay and then go eat some good Mexican food in the Mission. The weekend would be on me; you won't have to pay for a thing. Come on up to San Francisco, bro."*

They'd had a conflicted relationship for a while when he first moved in with his foster parents. In with Abby and her younger brother, Rick. Sean always felt that she resented the time the Sanchez family spent on him, her new "brother," or "so-called brother," as Abby called him, for at least a year, until she finally realized that Sean wasn't going away. But they were adults now, and that was way in the past; they had come to really respect and love each other. Still, he was not only surprised by her offer but also pleased.

He texted back a reply to her message: "Okay, you got me. But to be honest, I'm only turning 48. So, when and where?"

He hadn't had a good road trip since the desert when everything had gone kind of wrong, and that girl Erin had dominated his thoughts ever since. Maybe he'd fly up; rates were cheap right now.

Taking his motorcycle would mean at least two days of riding before he'd get there. He'd just sold a photograph, a funny one, of a desert mouse, tiny against the large moonlit landscape. He had a little extra money, and he thought it would be fun to fly. Abby wouldn't mind driving him around, and he could catch a bus ride to where she taught in the city. He'd look up flights and prices and make a plan later, after coffee. He wanted to call Abby, but he knew she would be teaching at the college and couldn't talk. Maybe he'd call her later on in the day when she'd be stuck in the inevitable traffic on Hwy 101 trying to get back from Marin County.

But what about MaeAnn? He had finally made a date with her and hoped there would be more than just one evening with her. Since their Thai dinner date was already planned, and it was still two weeks before his birthday, maybe if it all went well, he would just tell her about the Sanchez family and who Abby was to him, that is, if she was even interested. MaeAnn was someone he wanted to see more of, and he knew she would understand this trip.

When he thought of San Francisco, he remembered watching the sailboats scud across the bay. The winds were almost always good in the channel by the Golden Gate. He'd been out there himself a time or two after getting out of the service. Some of his fellow Marines, friends who were with him in the Middle East had bought small sailboats. They were racing them out of Berkeley Marina and he had gone up a few times to be a crew member. At least he knew how to duck to keep from getting hit on the head by the boom. He didn't much like competition, though. He preferred the solo time on a surfboard to hanging out low over the edge of a sailboat to help gain speed.

His foster sister Abby taught English as a Second Language at two community colleges and was able to share a place in San Francisco with a couple, both teachers. He hadn't told her about Erin yet, but she would be a good person to confide in. She liked a good puzzle to solve, and she was drawn to drama without making any kind of judgments. He laughed, thinking about the endless puzzle pieces he'd find when it was his turn vacuuming at the Sanchez household. They were his immediate family— his parents, sister, and brother—but in his own head, he would always think of them as the Sanchez family. He was an outsider, even though they never treated him like one. He would tell Abby everything, how he'd like to find this woman, how he was actively looking for Erin. She might have some good ideas for him. After all, she wrote in her spare time, and had even sold one murder mystery to a halfway decent publisher.

He got dressed and decided to go check in on MaeAnn and get his first coffee of the day. He hoped he wouldn't seem too eager now that he had gotten a yes from the pretty waitress. Still, it was his morning habit to go there for coffee and a pastry, so it wouldn't really seem different. And yet it was.

Chapter 12
Mothers

As she showered, she noticed a very thin stream of blood trickling down her leg. *God, maybe I'm having a miscarriage,* Elizabeth thought. She might not have to tell Najid if this were a miscarriage. She decided to just wait and see what happened by the end of the day. By her calculations, she would be about three months pregnant. She had read this was the most common time for a miscarriage.

"Shit," she said, throwing a pillow across the room and into the mirror of her antique dresser. This would be the day her period would be starting normally—she tracked it on her phone. A clever guy had figured that out. Why couldn't a woman have thought of it first? The menstrual cycle as a phone app. Now women felt comfortable discussing their cycles with men, but still, most men would rather not know anything about it. Except, of course, if it might inconvenience them in some way. *Like a pregnancy might,* she thought.

The strip from the kit lay on the bathroom counter, a faded pink now. She glanced at it and then threw it into the waste basket. She needed to get out and clear her head. She would ride over to the Asian Art Museum. There was an Islamic exhibit, Pearls on a String, that she'd been wanting to see. She still was able to afford her student discount membership. Maybe beauty was what she needed now. Najid was not around, or she could have met him there. She looked forward to seeing ancient art, not the kind made by Andy Warhol.

******

After an inspirational day surrounded by the kind of things she loved at the Asian Museum, she sat down and read through the first pages of her thesis. She was beginning to form an idea... how she could revise, and rename her paper, and how she would really show the wonders of the textiles of the ancient Orient. She could add in some graphics and maybe even turn it into a book. Now, anyone could create a book on the internet, and for hardly any money. She tucked her thesis back into its large manila envelope and placed it back into its new spot on the bookshelf above her desk. She should do some work today, but she was always so tired now that she was pregnant. She just fell asleep on her love seat and started to dream.

In her dream, Elizabeth was surrounded by colorful multiples of her mother, kind of like an Andy Warhol of Jackie O, or Marilyn Monroe, except that in real life, her mother looked nothing like either woman. In the dream, the Dr. was pointing to the images of her mother and saying, "She is dying; her cells are multiplying like crazy. Soon she'll be gone, and there is nothing for you to do but to carry on the family name. Elizabeth, you need to get pregnant."

"But," Elizabeth said to the Dr. in the dream, "I am pregnant now."

"Get pregnant again," the Dr. told her.

She woke up sweating in a hormone flush. What in the world did that dream mean? It meant that she was freaked out, and not only was she afraid of being a mother, but she was also afraid of her mother's continued power over her, even in death. Her mother had died on Elizabeth's 24th birthday. They'd said she had inoperable cancer and it would kill her, but Elizabeth knew that what was killing her mother were the secrets. The secrets others paid her to keep, and those of her own, had filled up all the spaces in her body until there was nothing of her left. No wonder in her dream, there were many mothers, all versions of the same mother. A therapist and a controlling mother who played the cello. A person unfathomable to Elizabeth, one made from quicksilver.

The dream left an unpleasant aftertaste. Or was it that Elizabeth needed to throw up? She raced for the bathroom. She didn't throw up; she just felt dizzy and let out a steady stream of pee, and when she wiped herself, there it was again, a spot of blood. Was this the way it was supposed to be when you were pregnant? She finally made an appointment to get a complete check-up. After all, she hadn't even dared to tell Najid yet. She was afraid of his response. The only thing she knew for sure was that pregnancy kits don't lie.

The next morning she seemed fine; no more blood, but still feeling woozy and queasy. She was sure the pregnancy had held. Mostly she felt relieved. Except for Najid; now, she had to tell him and it had to be in person. He would return later in the week from his latest trip, this one just to New York City.

Elizabeth texted him:

"Nej: Can you come here as soon as you get home? I feel the need to discuss something important with you." She had flung out the text before she made it sound better, less ominous, but she had done it fast before she lost the nerve for it.

He texted back, *"Of course, my love, I want to know what is important to you, maybe to us. I fly into SFO on Tuesday, and I will come right over."*

"Call first," she texted.

"I will if you want me to," he answered.

"Thank you, Nej."

She wanted to say more, and talk about the exhibit, but she was so tired all she could do was grab a book and lie down on her bed, and soon, she could hear herself snore softly. Naps seemed to be her habit now. Like all the cats she had owned, she could lie down anywhere to rest or read, and soon, she would be curled up asleep.

The next day, same; no blood and feeling sick and feeling exhausted. How do all these mothers all over the world do this? She hadn't expected this, she didn't really know what she had expected, but if her sister Deirdre were somewhere close, she could ask her. She was a mom, but Deirdre didn't answer her phone now, she knew Deirdre was not available.

She called Dr. Chong on Maria's recommendation and she was actually looking forward to finding out more about her pregnancy.

She liked Dr. Chong. *She was very relaxed, and she made Elizabeth relax—if that's how you can describe being on an examining table with legs spread and a speculum inside of you,* Elizabeth thought. Still, Dr. Chong was gentle and professional. "Elizabeth, I can tell by the color of your cervix that you are very pregnant. I would say over three months now. But we will measure you, and that will help us tell. Of course, you may know the date of conception?"

Elizabeth realized Dr. Chong was actually asking her for that information. "Yes, I think it might have been one night with unprotected sex. And that was about three and a half months ago."

Now this made Elizabeth ashamed. It made her seem incompetent, and that, she knew once again, was her mother talking to her. But Dr. Chong just said, "Okay then, with that date and how you look today and the way your breasts also look, and you say they are tender, we can say for sure that you have a baby in there, and actually, if you'd like we can do a sonogram today. I heard the heartbeat, but we could also take a look, and maybe, if you want to know, sometimes we can tell gender at this time. Do you want that?"

Elizabeth was not at all ready for this last question. She was quiet, and Dr. Chong just patted Elizabeth's belly and said, "It doesn't hurt at all, not you, and doesn't bother the fetus either."

"Okay, yes, yes," Elizabeth stammered, "Let's do it. Could you? What I'm saying is I'm fine with the sonogram, and also, if the gender is determined, I would like to know that as well."

"And," continued Dr. Chong, "some women of your age want to get an amniocentesis, to make sure the fetus is normal, without any real big problems. Do you want that?"

"NO!" said Elizabeth emphatically; she couldn't go that far. The sonogram was enough for today.

"Please wait a few minutes; we will need to set up the sonogram machine for your picture."

Ten minutes later, there it was on the screen, that tadpole, that strange little creature that was living and swimming around in

72

her womb. She couldn't stop the few tears that welled up. A mix of strange reality and the fact that she would be a mother and not that long from now.

"And you said you wanted to know if we can confirm a gender. Well, we do see the very beginnings of a penis, so guess what? Most likely a boy! We can confirm later on at the next ultra sound." The technician wheeled the machine away as Dr. Chong made notes on her laptop and then handed a print out of the sonogram to Elizabeth.

"Fine, then you may get dressed and make an appointment for next month. Also, you will need to start taking supplements for your pregnancy. And, I wonder, how do you feel about your pregnancy?"

Elizabeth paused and then said, "You know it's unexpected, but I am happy about it."

"Well then, congratulations to you. And what about the father?"

The father, oh now, she was hoping to dodge this one. She paused and then said,

"I haven't really told him yet, but I think he'll be happy too." Dr. Chong smiled and shook Elizabeth's hand, and left the room.

A boy, and now, the task of telling "the father," and hoping for the best all the way around. How would Najid feel? They were only getting to know each other, but they shared this baby.

When she was outside the building, she made a quick call to her friend Maria. Maria didn't answer but Elizabeth couldn't help herself, she left a message.

Guess what...I'm going to be a mother.

And a few seconds later.

Let's meet for coffee, and you can tell me everything. Love you, Maria.

Chapter 13
Lotus Flower

Steam from his coffee swirled up into the air, but Sean waited to take a first sip. He just wanted to see MaeAnn turn toward him and smile before he raised the cup to his lips. And she did. She gave Sean a small smile, the kind of smile that meant they shared a secret, and it was a good kind of secret. The coffee was strong and just what he counted on to wake up his mind. He had a lot to do now that he had made a call to Abby and had a date set for arrival in Oakland. She talked him into taking Amtrak up the coast, on the Coast Starlight. He would end up at Jack London Square in Oakland, and easy access to BART. He'd fly home. The idea of just sitting on a train and watching the scenery, the waves, and the pebbled beaches roll by without any pressure to deal with crowded Hwy 101 really appealed to him.

MaeAnn came over to top off his coffee, and he left his thoughts behind and paid full attention. "I'm looking forward to tomorrow night," she said, looking straight into Sean's eyes without any sign of nervousness.

He gazed back at her and said, "Me too, MaeAnn. Shall I pick you up, or if you live close like I do, we could walk down together."

"Let's just meet there," she said, "and just to be sure you understand, I will be paying for my own dinner, Sean."

"Okay, that's fine," he said. "Understood."

He didn't mind that she was starting out this date with a sense of control and independence; he admired that in women. He remembered in the military, most guys hated that in women. He didn't date much out of loyalty to the girl back in Palmdale, but she had broken his heart with a text message that simply said, "I'm sorry, Sean, I'm pregnant, and I'm getting married in a month. You'll always be my first love."

A huge shock after all he'd felt for her, the way he'd been with other women, trying to keep only to this girlfriend who obviously wasn't doing the same for him. That night he went to a whore house, surprised to find they existed in the Middle East, but where there are men, there will be sex for sale. He blushed as MaeAnn was still looking in his direction and smiling. Stop! he told his mind.

The week went quickly and it was the night of the big date. As he walked down the boardwalk, there she was, MaeAnn standing in front of Lotus Flower. She had on a flowered top, tight white pants, sandals that showed her toenails painted a bright red, and even with her hair partially clipped back, her black hair still hung down practically as he had imagined, to her waist. He was stunned. She was waving and smiling, and he waved back. He hoped he looked okay, he had on his best clothes, long beige dockers, and a short-sleeved striped shirt, which could have used a little pressing, but he didn't even own an iron. He wore a new pair of Vans and had a green sweater slung over his shoulder. The fog could come in later, and he had almost a mile walk to home. He might need the sweater, but right now, it was causing him to sweat.

When he caught up with her, he said, "You look so different without your black T-shirt, dark pants, and denim apron," She gave him a look, and he said more, "MaeAnn, you look beautiful."

"Ha ha, thanks," she said, "You look different too without those baggy shorts and *Hoagie Boards* T-shirt you always wear."

"*Manatee Surf Shop Hoagie T-shirt*, and it's my favorite shirt. I found it online. It's vintage from the 60s. Vintage, you know, kind of like me."

They walked into the restaurant, and a young host showed them to a table toward the back. It was cool and on the dark side. A fake waterfall surrounded by orchids, a Buddha near the base. Sean shrugged; it would be fine here. The food was always good, and he knew this place and the host. He pulled out MaeAnn's chair and sat down across from her.

"How old are you, Sean?" MaeAnn asked

"As I said, I'm vintage too, turning forty-eight very soon. And you?"

She looked puzzled for a minute, and then laughed. "I'm thirty-one, but people always think I'm younger. My skin, courtesy of my parents from the Philippines; fewer wrinkles."

"Well, I'm glad you're at least that old," Sean said, "I was afraid you were going to say twenty and too young for me!"

She laughed, and he liked the sound of it.

They ordered, surrounded by what he considered beach trappings: tiki torches, surfboards on the walls, woody wagon tea light holders, a small orchid on each table. They talked about mundane beach things. They named their favorite beaches; he told her the best places to surf and about Laird Hamilton riding waves as big as skyscrapers. MaeAnn said that she liked the way women were finally being invited to Mavericks. Then they talked about how there were wild fires all up and down the state right now. Sean felt comfortable with her, and his head didn't hurt like it often did on a first date. They had tropical drinks and ordered them, "no little umbrellas, please."

"You know it's almost my birthday and my foster sister, Abby, just invited me up to San Francisco to celebrate. She thinks I'm turning fifty! And she wants me to come by train, the Coast Starlight."

"So you're from a foster family?"

"It's a long story, so I won't bore you, but yes, they were a good family, and they basically saved me. And Abby is the one I'm still close to. My foster parents are gone now. Both died about two years ago."

"I'd like to know more about your family, Sean, but for starters, tell me a little about Abby."

Sean was glad, the safer part of his family history. "Abby is my older foster sister, and she's organic to the max. She makes green drinks, her own yogurt, she buys raw wool and dyes it in big vats placed around her apartment. There's always sheep's hair and color everywhere. She teaches at two community colleges. I guess the best way I can describe her is messy, colorful and concerned about staying healthy and saving the planet."

"Ha, ha, sounds like someone I would like, but she's picked a very big job!"

"She's the one who has always been there for me. My foster parents, too, of course. They raised me from the time I was five."

"I'm from an ocean-loving family," MaeAnn said. "First the Philippines, then Hawaii, then here. They always hoped I'd go to college, but I started waiting tables and sketching in my free time, and now I just want to do art and wait tables. I'm like my mom too; I like to get my hands into dirt."

Sean mapped out a little more of his life, and ended with his stint as a medic. His wounds. He hadn't meant to say anything about that, but she seemed to want to know all about him and he didn't often have the chance to talk to people like this, talk in a deeper way.

"Wow," she said, "that all sounds like a wild ride, no wonder you love to surf. But the train ride, taking the Coast Starlight, that's scenic for a lot of the way, until it heads inland, and it takes you right through the Air Force base."

"Vandenberg," he said, "yes, right by the space platforms. If I'm lucky, I'll see a shot."

"If you're lucky, you won't. I once took that train up to Santa Barbara, and we were delayed two hours; the train was not allowed to enter the base during a space shot. Still, the trail the missile left behind lit up the sky hours later and became part of an amazing Santa Barbara sunset. For me, that made up for the delay. And you won't have to deal with the 101 or airport security."

"Oh, I'm flying back into San Diego," Sean said, "I got a special deal. Anyway, I'd like to see you again," he told her over green papaya salad.

"I'd like that," MaeAnn said.

Their dinner came and went, and later Sean couldn't even remember much of what they ate. He only remembered her face, her smile and her great laugh and how he could imagine waking up in bed with her.

"Why didn't you ever become an EMT? From what you've told me today about being a medic, you have all the training for it," MaeAnn said.

"No more blood and crisis for me, no more grieving families."

"I can understand," she said, "but I'll bet you'd be someone I would want to have come to my rescue in an emergency."

He laughed, but then she said, "No, I really mean it; you're a person people can trust right away." She took the last bite of her rice dessert, and he took the last sip of his Singha beer.

Even though he'd insisted on paying for their dinner, she had protested, "No way, I'm happy to pay for mine. Remember?"

They each paid their bill while she smiled at him. He nodded his head; yes, he understood. He trusted her and felt she would be an important person in his life, he saw it clearly. And she would trust him with her life. She had said so. He took her hand across the table and squeezed it.

They went outside on a particularly starry summer night. They saw a few shooting stars. "August the Perseus Meteor Showers," Sean said. They held hands and just watched the night sky from a block away where it was darker, and then suddenly, she kissed him and said, "Thank you Sean, I want to see you again and I hope I see you before your trip." She turned abruptly and left him standing speechless and tingling. Something had started here that he might just be ready for. He thought she felt the same. He couldn't carry a tune, but there was no one to hear so as he walked back to his apartment he sang. Don McLean. Like all the vintage things he liked, the music was old, but he knew all the lyrics.

Starry Night, starry, starry night

78

Paint your palette blue and gray
Look out on a summer's day
With eyes that know the darkness in my soul.

Vincent Van Gogh's work always swirled through his mind too... the amber wheat fields, the sunflowers, the water, the star-filled skies.

The fog was pulling in, and he tugged his sweater over his head. The stars were getting dimmer and dimmer, but he knew they were still there, along with the planets. They just kept going around and around.

Chapter 14
Deirdre's Fall

She could barely stand now, but she was being made to walk down a long hallway. It was so dark; Deirdre had been ordered to remove everything, all her jewelry, and except for the lab coat and underwear, all the rest of her clothes including her shoes.

When she entered the room, forcefully guided by a man in a black uniform. She saw that it was set up for surgery with infusion equipment, boxes of sterile bandages, bags of fluids, picc lines and bright overhead lights. She had to blink a minute so her eyes could adjust and then she saw two nurses, one of them a woman, their faces covered with surgical masks. "Take off that lab coat and lie down on this gurney." She did as she was told. Trembling from fear and from cold, she was covered with a sheet.

What the hell was happening to her? She'd not expected anything like this, ever. Even if what she did could sometimes be dangerous, it was not this kind of danger. The danger she usually faced was from bugs, disease, poisonous snakes or plants, men with machetes after jewelry, or guys guarding big plantations. Not this, not what was happening to her now. She knew how to deal with the other dangers, but not *this* kind.

She saw that needles were being poked into her arms. Her brain was already fuzzy from a drink she'd been given first—and then she heard the start of a drip. She just heard someone say, "Put that over her face," and... nothing more. All she heard was a ticking sound. Her heart, she decided.

Eventually she was asked something—where something was.

Where? Where?

But she couldn't answer, she couldn't even form a word with her lips. She heard someone say, "She's not responding, let's just use the other drug on her and get this over with." And then again, blackness.

Then she was falling. She felt herself jerk to avoid a cliff and then, she fell again, and again and again.

A nightmare again, the same over and over. She wiped sweat from her forehead and sat up in bed taking a big drink of cold water.

When would it ever stop? she wondered.

Chapter 15
Persian Love Cake

Elizabeth couldn't sleep. She missed Najid, and she was still feeling very conflicted about the baby. She walked over and took down the book of Persian poets and turned to Hafez:

forget your voice, sing forget your feet, dance
forget your life, live, forget yourself, and be.

She had the baby in her belly; she had the sonogram to prove it, and most likely, it would be a little boy. Now, how to tell the father of this baby? Elizabeth was tempted to just email the sonogram of their son, but that wouldn't be right. She needed to talk to him and hear what he had to say about this pregnancy. She was scared, but felt the urge to just get up in the morning and call him.

The phone rang and rang, and finally went to his phone message. She did not want to leave a message, so she just hung up, but minutes later her cell chimed and she saw it was Najid.

"Hello, Betta, I see you have called me. The rare occurrence," he said laughing.

"Yes, I know, I hate to call you during your work day, but this is something that just couldn't wait."

"Okay, I hope it's a good something that just can't wait."

"I think it is, but since it's been a shock to me, it may be to you as well."

"Well let's have it," Najid said with a soft laugh.

"I'm pregnant. It's for sure. I have a sonogram and I have heard the baby's heart beat."

Her own heart pounded. Sweat broke out; she felt it dampen her breasts. He was taking forever to respond. Finally, he coughed and cleared his throat.

"This is the best news ever," he said, "now I have to make you dinner and you must come over with the picture of our baby." Then it sounded like he was blowing his nose.

"Sorry," he said, "this news has made me cry a little. Don't worry it is a happy cry."

"Call me later when you can?"

"Yes, we will make a date to talk about this important development. I am excited, Betta, I really am."

She was finally able to breathe. He meant it, meant that he was okay with the pregnancy. He would be a part of this. Now she had to embrace this pregnancy too, and drive away any last minute doubts she had about the rightness of going forward with this pregnancy.

She let out a big sigh.

Najid came over at end of that week and they talked through half the night until she fell asleep in his arms. Inadvertently, he had spent the whole night with her in her bed. They curled together, and she liked it.

In the morning after each had showered she made them oatmeal with brown sugar and milk. He sat down and took a bite.

"Right now I feel King of the Mountain," he said looking at her.

Then he told Elizabeth that he would be gone for three weeks and he wasn't sure how often he could be in touch, he would be in some remote areas with sketchy cell service. They finished their breakfast and they walked out of her place together, Elizabeth waved to a curious neighbor on the sidewalk. Najid and Elizabeth hugged, a long hug, with a warmth she had never felt coming from him before. And she realized she felt something spark as they touched. They had created a baby, and this lit up a deeper part of her. One that had been dormant for a long time.

Three weeks seemed an eternity. With Najid traveling and Elizabeth still feeling a little queasy, she sat and read books on pregnancy that her friend Maria brought over. Maria was older with a lot of experience when it came to babies! She also had a call from a grad school friend; there was a careful outdoor meet-up happening next week. No one would have to wear masks. She could look forward to that.

She went for long walks in the city, or rode her scooter to get groceries, skirting the areas that were always filled with tents. The grad school gathering turned out to be just what she needed to get her thinking seriously about her thesis.

Najid texted: *"When I'm home on Thursday, finally, I want to treat you to a Persian meal at my place."* He gave his address on Green Street and basic directions. Today her phone rang and she quickly picked it up.

"Hello, my sweet. I hope you are feeling well now. Did you get my message about our meal together at my place? I know you are going to love this food, my Betta, and it will be good for our little growing bean as well. I look forward to serving you a meal from my country. And at the end I will serve you some Persian Love Cake."

"A Persian Love Cake?"

"Yes, it is said that each bite is filled with love and with each bite you fall deeper and deeper in love."

For a moment she couldn't speak. Such tenderness and care, something she hadn't experienced with men before. She took an audible breath which he must have heard on his end,

"Betta are you okay?"

"Yes I am more than okay. Thank you, Najid. I'll see you on Thursday. Oh, and what time?" she asked.

"Make it 7:00. I will have the meal in the oven and some things to serve you when you walk in my door. I have to go now, but I will see you soon. Remember you can call me Nez."

She heard his phone click off and reluctantly she hung up. Najid—well, Nez now—would be back, and finally she would see his place and he was making a meal for her. It all sounded too good to be true. But somehow, she still couldn't find comfort in the nickname he requested. Maybe in time.

"Thunk thunk thunk," the little brass fist announced her presence. She knew many people in the city still had these really old door knockers.

"Please, come in." Najid said opening the heavy carved door. When she saw the cacophony of color and metal that was his home she was astounded. His place so very different from hers. She thought he'd probably brought these fine things with him from Iran, but he did not explain much. He was evasive when it came to explanations of what exactly he did to earn a living or why he traveled so much.

"So now you see it," he said, with a sweeping arm motion towards the many decorative items scattered across carved tables and dressers. Wooden animals, brass candlesticks, embroidered pillows, mirrors with tiled borders, so much. And in the other room she could see his bed with its filigreed brass headboard. Elizabeth wondered how many other Americans had these treasure chests emptied out into their rooms.

She plopped her backpack down on an ottoman, and took out the sonogram, shyly putting it on top of her pack. Later, she thought, after the meal, not now.

His flat, this cave of colors and cloth--overlapping Kilim rugs on the floor, tapestries on the walls, and one wall of photos. Brass teapots and a pile of yet more rugs in the corner.

"For you," he said, handing her a glass. "Pomegranate juice," he said as she was still trying to get a better look at the bed.

She carefully took the glass of juice. She didn't want to spill anything here. Still she couldn't resist running her free hand along the lime green velvet of Najid's couch. She liked its soft but firm texture. As she walked around from one object to the next she sipped her sweet drink.

How little effort she put into her own place, her treasures kept out of sight in a trunk in her narrow hallway. Her purchases from India and Pakistan still nestled in their wrapping papers, except for her favorite pink paisley scarf. Recently she'd unearthed an appliquéd top decorated with elephants and palm trees that would work when her belly grew big. "Fitting, the elephant images," she'd said to Maria when she'd tried it on. It was loose but in another month or two would be perfect. Both she and Maria had a long laugh over the elephants.

She looked back into the kitchen, and in the corner she saw a colorful cake. *It must be the love cake*, she thought. *Funny*, she thought, *I'm blushing over a love cake.*

Najid had the kettle on to boil water for their tea and retrieved a honey jar from the cupboard; he knew by now that she liked her tea sweetened. He picked up the brass teapot with matching small cups and put them on a tray. The way he did it was not fussy, but practiced. So familiar to him, she thought, just as normal as her brewing an espresso at her place and taking down her favorite mug from a wooden rack.

She walked over to the wall of photos, mostly black and white. There were several of groups of men and women together in what she assumed was traditional attire. The color photos showed off embroidery and brocades, purple, green and blue hues, dangling necklaces on the women, head turbans for the men, and turbans even worn by some of the women. There were more, including one that seemed to be Najid in a cap and gown, and the women in that picture, wearing hijabs. It struck her as such a contrast. The rich colors and textures of the old costumes, and then the drabness of the dark chador garb. The newer government, religion.

There was one picture that struck her so powerfully that she stopped in front of it and stared. A woman with long black hair, large dark eyes, and an angular, appealing face. She was holding a child with a halo of very dark curls in her arms. There was something beautiful yet sad about this picture. Najid came over and started pointing out people in the pictures to the side of this woman, explaining, "These are uncles, cousins, this one smiling is

86

my mother. My maman, is getting pretty fragile now. She is over eighty, and has been through so many changes." He told a funny story about his brother and how much they looked alike and how they used to play tricks on girls when they were in their teens. Nothing was said about the woman, or the child she held. Elizabeth went back to stand in front of the one picture. Najid came over and put his arm around her. Finally, when she looked at him he said,

"My wife and my daughter."

"You have a wife and a child," she said angrily, pulling his arm from around her waist and staring at him with barely contained rage. She waited for an explanation. But Najid bowed his head and when he raised his face to her, she saw that tears streamed down his check. He quickly wiped his eyes, his face. *He is about to give me some apologetic BS story,* she thought, and this made her furious. With hands on her hips she demanded, "Okay, let me hear it right now!"

"They're gone now. A market bombing when we were in Pakistan on business. I can say no more." He turned away from her and went into the kitchen. He turned off the whistling kettle, which was screaming by now, and poured water into the pot, and then poured it out again, and re-poured water onto the tea leaves. He took out a large tray of kebobs from the refrigerator. They were both silent. She sat down in a nearby chair, pillows cushioning her. She showed now, a little tummy at over four months. *And, to think it took this long before I find out about a wife, and a different child,* she thought. A tragedy too. She found herself crying softly and she tried to hide the sounds, but Najid heard anyway and turned back toward her from the stove.

"You are my love," he said, "and this baby—now you can see—means more to me than you can ever imagine." That just made her cry harder. He came over to the chair with the tray which he set down as he handed her a cup of tea and a kissed her forehead.

"Don't be sad," he said, "I think of them as in heaven now."

Oh, she didn't know what to think. She didn't believe in heaven, even though she'd always wished that she did.

This man was slowly revealing himself to her. She looked down at the floor, at the rich red, purple, and brown rug below her and noticed the *Persian Tree of Life* symbol, drawing heaven and earth together. She recognized it from her studies. *It also could stand for the placenta,* she thought. She took another sip of tea and watched Najid put the chicken kabobs in the oven to heat and then start a pot of rice. He said he would surprise her and he had, in so many ways. He turned to her and said, "Typical Persian meal, chicken kabob, rice with cardamom and other spices, vegetable, eggplant with yogurt. I hope you like it. Oh, and most important of all, a slice of Persian Love Cake." He smiled. They had finished with tears now.

"Elizabeth," he said, "so far, you are one of the few people who've come here into my home, my sanctuary which reminds me of my other home and life so far away. I'm relieved that you've seen the picture of Zara and my little Sonja. I did not want to keep this from you, but now, with you pregnant and seeming to want me in your life, I had to share it. That little family was quite a few years ago and now I'm ready to take the chance of loving again."

"Nej, it's a boy; we are going to have a son." She picked up the sonogram and handed to him.

"I can't look at this just yet." He set it down near the table. "Maybe after dinner." She understood.

"Come, let's eat together and talk about all of it." He smiled as he set the food on his small table in the dining nook. He helped her up and pulled out a cushioned rosewood chair.

"Someday, I'd like to take you to Iran, to my Persia, and let you indulge yourself in the best foods there, and see the rich colors of everything Persian. And we will see the places with the symbols of my religion."

He came back to the table with an engraved brass platter filled to the top with rice dotted with pomegranate seeds, almonds, raisins and oranges. "Jeweled Rice," Najid said as he spooned some out onto her plate.

And in the kitchen she saw it again, the Persian Love Cake topped with what appeared to be rose petals and pistachios. She picked up a brass fork and dug into the rice and smiled as the first pomegranate seed fired open in her mouth. She really felt that she would never be able to duplicate this moment. A yearning had been satisfied, and she had a taste for even more of the same from this man. And the baby; all was unfolding in front of her, like a silk robe, like an old silk fan.

Chapter 16
Coast Starlight

Sean had his canvas duffle on the bed and was trying to figure out what to take with him to Northern California, with its unpredictable skies, the weather in June often overcast. He had seen the fog pour over the Golden Gate as he walked across the bridge his last visit. On his skin the damp air felt soft, different from the prickly feel of rain.

He threw in his one slightly tattered thick sweater, a couple of jeans, his favorite shorts, swim trunks, tees, Jockey briefs, and one pair of socks, although he mostly would wear his Vans without socks. He grabbed his leather jacket and brought his smaller good camera with its leather carrying case. It was just so much better than his phone camera. *There*, he thought, *he had everything. Oh and a face mask too, depending on current restrictions.*

As he ran to the station, he felt it was worth being a little tight on the schedule because he'd taken time to go by the Tidal Wave and say goodbye to MaeAnn. They'd kissed in front of everyone and he felt so happy that she liked him enough to do that. A "PDA", she'd told him: public display of affection. He held up his phone to show his ticket and climbed on. Since the train was leaving from the San Diego station, there were still plenty of empty seats. He knew that sometimes these Starlights were standing room only. Although now, fewer people were traveling.

As the train started up it was louder than he expected and the movement past the stationary train next to his made him slightly dizzy. He closed his eyes and pressed on the sea bands he always wore when he was on a boat, a plane, a train, anything where the motion was not a wave or his own feet or a motorcycle. Quickly, the train's speed caught up to the cars driving the freeways of San Diego and then it seemed to be going faster as it switched over closer to the coast. The train sounded its horn going through the coastal towns. He imagined the sound in these towns, haunting, bouncing off the foothills. As he watched out the window, he made mental notes of places where he thought he could get good photos later. He had sold one more photo at the gallery in Los Angeles and had gotten the check just in time for this trip. The popular one of wolves. *That was a lucky break,* he thought.

The hills were yellow with wildflowers, the last remnants of the spring "super bloom". Rain, then sun, in California. This year the welcome rain lasting through mid-July. This moment on the train made him smile. The hills, first parched from the drought, and then black from wild fires, now a velvety green.

The Starlight was rolling along at a steady pace, the scenery unfolding, and Sean in a bit of a dreamy mood until he realized what he needed was some strong coffee. He took his camera and his small back pack with him to the lounge car. Balancing carefully as he walked down the long aisles he finally reached the car with its coffee, pastries, Dunkin' Doughnuts, and a full breakfast cooked in the train's kitchen. He sat down and looked over the menu. When the porter came he ordered scrambled eggs, orange juice, and, of course, his coffee—black. As much as he was tempted, he decided to forgo a doughnut. Sugar and Sean were not a good mix.

People were ambling into the dining car. Hungry families with kids, lots of single travelers. He'd wanted to sit by himself, but saw it wasn't possible, and soon he was talking, well mostly listening, to a chatty girl who was returning home after a year at college in San Diego. He found it easy to let her do most of the talking. He just smiled occasionally and nodded and asked a question that would get her going again. He knew it was easier for him to listen than to talk.

Her name was Rebecca and she had completed her freshman year at UCSD. He was impressed with her light spirit and her ability to say how she felt about the current political situation with so many unwilling to listen to scientists. She wanted to be a Dr., but was also interested in robotics. He only shared one brief story about his time as a medic in Afghanistan and she frowned and nodded as he spoke of the injuries there.

"Prosthetics, that's another interest of mine," she said, at the end of his story. "I want to help these injured people. Oh, this is my stop. Bye Sean, nice talking with you," she said getting up and quickly walking away.

He couldn't believe that artificial limbs would be what any young person would like to study and then, possibly, design, but then they were all brought up on video games with creatures made like transformers, a ship becoming a giant superhero or a spider-like creature. *Ah,* he thought, *but they know nothing of real war.* He shuddered, grabbed an orange from the serving bar for later on and walked back to his seat. Before he could even look at the change of direction, away from the ocean and toward inland California, he felt his eye lids closing.

He woke with a start from a dream of flinging out his arms and then trying to fly after being blown into the air by a bomb. He wiped sweat away and got out the orange, carefully peeling it and separating the segments like his foster mother had taught him a long time ago, before she got sick and couldn't talk anymore. He finished the orange, which wasn't as sweet or juicy as he'd have liked, and cleaned his hands with a wipe from his backpack. Taking his camera out he focused in on the hills. The pictures could be blurry, but he just wanted the suggestion of hills anyway. He clicked away.

After a dinner, and what seemed like miles and miles of fairly uninteresting scenery, with only cotton fields, rows of strawberries, and the odd rusted truck to photograph as the train headed toward Oakland. He took BART to San Francisco.

After walking to the Ferry Building he found a warm spot to sit. Like a cat, Sean was always drawn to a sunny spot. He sipped his Peet's Coffee espresso and watched people stroll by, not as many tourists, but still a steady stream. Suddenly a woman caught his eye. Her hair, a light red, and curly, the color his foster mother would have called strawberry blond. In the breeze, the ends of a

92

pashmina scarf lightly danced around her as she strolled along. He looked more closely; it was pink with paisleys and he believed it was a match to the one the woman in the desert had clutched in her hand. When this woman was in front of him she gave him a smile, and he took a better look at the scarf. Waving to her and smiling back, he tried to stay calm. But he was sure it was identical to the one on the blond woman in the desert that he had found months ago. He'd been told that by his therapist that his visual memory was strong.

Should he say something? It was not his usual style to strike up a conversation of any kind with a stranger, but she looked friendly. He wanted to know about the scarf, with it's rosy paisleys, but he had to be cautious. He didn't want her to think he might be some kind of creep. But for him in this moment, it was all about the scarf. He flashed back to the desert, to the rose tattoo, the stillness and pale skin of the unidentified blond he had come across. Where was she? All he knew was that her name was Erin and she was a botanist. Was she alright? He ached to know how she'd fared after leaving the hospital in Palmdale. His head started to throb. The woman looked at him. He knew he was getting pale and sweaty,

"Are you okay?" she asked. When she turned toward him he saw that she was very pregnant.

"Just a little sea sick from that," he pointed toward the ferry boat. A simple white lie, he assured himself.

The woman looked over; it was true that the bay was particularly choppy. "Oh," she said, "do you need anything?"

He wiped sweat away with his pocket bandanna. "I like your scarf, " Sean said, looking again at the pashmina. She said, "It's my favorite, from Pakistan. I lived there for awhile, but it was a gift."

As Sean was about to ask more, a man, tall and dark, probably her husband by the way they smiled at each other, came along and took her elbow. He nodded at Sean, and they walked on. Sean was shaken not only by the scarf and the woman, but by the man. He looked so familiar, like many men he had seen in Iraq, in Pakistan. The guy definitely didn't want to stick around Sean, and with a grip on her elbow, he seemed to almost push her forward along the sidewalk. Sean noticed that she turned toward him and gently removed his hand from her elbow as they continued to walk away.

Before he had time to think about it, he heard his name being called. It was his sister Abby coming toward him waving her hand back and forth like a fast moving pendulum. He grabbed his duffle and walked toward Abby as she ran the last bit of the way. She threw her arms around him.

"I've missed you so, Sean, it's great to see you. You look tanned and fit, and, well, pretty relaxed."

He worked to let go of the tension that had built up around his interaction with the woman, and her husband. and simply said, "Thank you, Abby. You look great yourself!" She gave a big hearty laugh. Her dark hair now had stands of silver in it and he really did think she looked good.

"Come on, let's find some paella and some agua fresca. Pretend we're in Spain," Abby said, taking Sean's arm. He patted her hand. She'd always been affectionate, once they finally got to know each other. Abby would probably have every minute planned for them; that's how she operated in the world, so different from his own free style. But sometimes he liked that about her. He didn't have to do much planning, she would take care of that.

Not like with most brothers and sisters who are born together, he had just kind of come along. "The charity case," as she'd called him a few times at the beginning. As they got to know each other, a certain kind of love developed, and he always thought of her as the one he could depend on. She had been a good support to him when he first returned with all his wounds healing, some hidden, some obvious.

They walked around the inside of the building that hosted a thriving market on this late afternoon. "We could go hear some good music tonight, if you want," she said.

He nodded; it would be more for her than for him, but he was glad to be with her wherever they decided to go. "What about your shopping?" Sean asked.

"Ah, I went earlier in the day near my work, let's just let someone else do the cooking for us."

She gave him a warm smile and he said, "Sure, that sounds like a really good idea. You know I love paella—or even Indian food would be good. Or heck, even a fish sandwich." They both laughed because here there were so many choices and they each recognized the love for food in one another.

That night at Abby's, Sean slept pretty well until around 3 a.m. in the morning when he thought he heard the latch click. He got out his phone and was ready to turn on the flashlight when he heard the door to his sister's room open and close. He waited.

Should he get up? Maybe there was a prowler in the neighborhood, or worse. He could feel the adrenaline pumping through his body. Then he heard soft voices talking together and the sound of sheets rustling. He thought he recognized the voice as Jason, her sister's former lover. Still Sean couldn't help himself; he walked to her door and just as he was about to knock, Abby suddenly opened it and walked out.

"I knew you'd be up. I know how you have super sensitive hearing and radar and all, and well, I just wanted to say, don't worry. It's Jason. He says he just missed me and I'm going to let him spend the night here. Jason will leave first thing, probably before either of us get up. It's all good, Sean. Tomorrow, we'll go to the Mission district for special fish tacos. Good night, dear brother. Sleep tight and don't let the bedbugs bite," she giggled and went back into her room.

He thought he could hear very subdued lovemaking going on in there, and it made him jealous. He wanted that, and he wanted it with MaeAnn.

Chapter 17
Blossoms

Elizabeth plucked a banana out of the fruit bowl. She'd relied on bananas in the first months of her pregnancy. They helped her through morning sickness. Not everything tasted the same to her now that she was pregnant. Bananas still tasted good. Coffee—not so good. But now she was seven months along, and with the earlier bleeding and scare of miscarriage behind her, she felt reassured with every kick she felt, with every move the baby made. Any lingering feelings she'd had that the baby was like an alien that had taken her over were now gone. He was her baby boy.

Elizabeth went outside and sat on the bench she and Najid had bought so that they could sit together in her little back yard. It still smelled of cedar. She ran her hand over the wood. Someone had carefully sanded it smooth. She pulled up her T-shirt and let the sun shine on her belly. "Here, sweetie, some California sunshine to make you strong."

She regularly talked to the baby. She called the bump "Babar " and "Tamir" and teased Najid with silly names like "Little Daisy," "Peanut," and "Booboo." He didn't mind. He just liked to feel the bump and her breasts and take her into the bedroom. "I love your full breasts and our little Najid Jr. in that belly of yours." He was playful, but he made her feel the power of being a pregnant woman. It amazed her how much she loved his company, his body, his affection and his sweet talk. She was just a fool and partly a slut for the attention, and the delicious sensuality of this man. The way he could run his hands all over her body as if she were a Persian cat. And he loved to lay his hand on her belly, waiting to feel a kick. And the way he whispered to her in his language, and as he said, the language of love. The Persian spell had been cast.

Today Elizabeth was thinking about her sister, about how they had shared the same bedroom and had looked at the same red roses on the same walls for years, until their mother remarried. But the trade-off—a new fancy bedroom and her own space at 14—for a stepfather who hit her mother in the next room hadn't been worth the price.

The ordeal had continued for four years until Elizabeth left for college. Her sister had left for university the year before, going in on perfect SAT scores and 4.0 plus grades, her amazing achievements getting her a full scholarship to Boston University. Elizabeth knew that her sister's successful nerdiness allowed her to ignore the nest of snakes that was called home.

Deirdre had always been a nut for plants. She was a walking encyclopedia of rare and endangered plants, had published an article already at 16. "Ten Plants That Can Kill You and Ten That Can Save You." Elizabeth had read it for errors, but there were none that she could find. Her sister's brilliance amazed and angered Elizabeth. She wished she had gotten some of that dedication and delight.

Elizabeth thought she had her share of passion, even if she didn't have the same drive to see things to a conclusion, to actually finish something, anything. That might change with this child, she thought to herself.

After her sister left for Boston, their mother went back to school, finishing up the college degree she had started before marriage and two little girls changed her direction. She also left Tom, and this pleased the sisters immensely. Elizabeth recalled the phone message that had awaited her years ago: "The bastard is gone, and all of his muddy shoes and stupid suits, and bottles of gin, gone too. I knew you'd want to know."

Elizabeth saw that her phone was blinking. A message. She went to her phone messages and there was the sound of Deirdre's voice. "I'm fine; I'm out of the hospital and recovering, so don't worry about me and don't listen to what our cousin has to say about me." But as to be expected, nothing more, no real way to contact her. None of the phone numbers she had for her sister worked and the one on this message was out of service when she re-dialed.

Elizabeth made some chamomile tea and sat and played the message again. Hearing her sister say the word "hospital," made her tense up so much that Elizabeth got a big cramp in her thigh. Deirdre had told her that she would be out of touch due to her new "highly classified job." Of course Deirdre could have called her; she wasn't sure why she hadn't, but she could be like that. Like their mother, Deirdre was someone who knew how to hide. She was secretive, and often, it seemed to Elizabeth, unhappy, despite her successes in the world of botany. She seemed happiest at her wedding, and then when her little boy was born years before. But Elizabeth cared about her sister and right now, she was determined to find her.

She brought up Google and typed in her sister's name as it had shown on her phone screen, Deirdre Erin Connelly. And what came up was her sister's picture with a cell phone number. She sent a text and it seemed to go through... "I'm pregnant, Deirdre, call me." *That ought to elicit a response*, she thought, tossing the banana skin into the garbage can by the door. She could still hit a basket or a can. This little kid inside her will be coordinated. She imagined them riding along together on their bikes going up the side of Mt. Tam.

She copied her sister's cell phone contact into her phone list and headed for a shower. She burst into song, David Bowie's, "Dancing in the Street," as she stepped under the water, shampoo sliding down her breasts and over her bump. Over little Bahar. As she was throwing on a very large top and clumsily pulling on a pair of elastic waist pants she noticed her cell phone light was blinking once again. A message from Deirdre, with a phone number ID.

"A baby, I wish I were pregnant again. Love you, Deirdre." Elizabeth read the message a second time. Suddenly she smiled at the thought of them in their rose-papered bedroom talking about their babies of the future and what their names would be: Rosie, Tucker, Charlie, Hampster, and Bowie. Their favorites in the 1990s.

As she was adjusting her clothes over her big belly, her cell phone rang in the kitchen. She quickly walked in and picked up. Maybe it would be her sister.

When she looked, Najid's name appeared on her screen. She answered the phone.

"How is Mommy today?" he asked.

"Getting fatter and sassier." she said. "Where are you?"

"I'm at the airport, just leaving for a few days, going back to D.C."

"Oh, I didn't know you'd be gone this week. Well, safe travels. Should be beautiful blossom time. I'm kind of jealous."

"Next time, my love, you will come with me." Elizabeth was intrigued and also conflicted. She didn't really understand how she felt about his travels, about not really knowing exactly what he did. Still, she'd love to be there with him now, seeing cherry blossoms. Elizabeth was drying her hair with one hand and holding the phone with her other hand and smiling like a fool remembering the nights two months ago after she'd been to Najid's flat and told him about the baby, the boy baby, he'd come over and read to her from the book of poetry he had given her. She opened the book and read from Rumi:

> The springtime of Lovers has come,
> that this dust bowl may become a garden;
> the proclamation of heaven has come,
> that the bird of the soul may rise in flight.
> The sea becomes full of pearls,
> the salt marsh becomes sweet as kauthar,
> the stone becomes a ruby from the mine,
> the body becomes wholly soul.

He'd read it aloud to her for a few nights in a row. *He just had to see her more than ever now*, she thought.

She was really surprised by his affection and already crazy nicknames for the multiplying mass of cells in her uterus. Their baby. Najid Jr, was a running joke, but then Little Bahar, the last one, his favorite, meaning spring.

"I love you, Elizabeth," Najid said before he hung up.

"M—me too," she stuttered out the words, always hard for her to say, like a cough that you just can't loosen. And then she added, "We'll miss you."

Already the baby and she had become a "we".

"Me too," Najid said. And the sound of a kiss over the phone. A kiss back before she clicked off.

She wondered what he really spent his time doing? But he never gave her much more than "It's a business trip," or "I don't want to bother you with these kind of details." It made her feel that he didn't think she could understand or was not interested, or he was just being skittish and secretive. She wasn't really ready for more secretive people in her life. She was done with secrets now that she'd told him about the baby.

She wanted everything out in the open, clear and direct. She wasn't sure she would get that with Najid. He had kept the dark secret of the bombing of that first family for months, and she was still trying to know how to feel about that. She wondered if he trusted her. She might not fully trust him.

As she slipped into bed and tried to read, she fell sound asleep. In her dream, she was wearing a white dress and veil and she was carrying the rose and lily bouquet. Najid stood waiting for her at the alter with two little kids, a dark girl about four years old and a two-year-old toddler wearing a name tag, Bahar. The little boy was twisting around uncomfortably to better see his mother walking down the aisle. When she came a little closer, he broke free from his father and raced to grab Elizabeth by the skirts, begging to be picked up. But she couldn't pick him up without dropping her bouquet, so they hobbled down the aisle together until Najid reached down and swooped him up, the little boy, fussing, until Najid set him back down and the dark child took his hand and shushed him. The girl was the one she had seen laughing in several pictures at Najid's place. Her name was Sonja—his

100

daughter, who would always be four. She wore Elizabeth's pink paisley scarf, and it swirled around her until she was practically mummified by it, the pink all she saw now as she hurried to take her vows. Suddenly she was taking her Catholic vows and taking a husband in the church and it wasn't Najid but some other man who walked with a slight limp. Najid vaporized with the two children leaving Elizabeth standing alone, holding her bouquet, which had turned into a mass of spaghetti noodles.

She was startled awake by the dream when she thought about that scarf; she hadn't seen it for months, hadn't worn it either. She dumped drawers out on her bed, frantically digging through for the scarf. Finally, in with her socks and leggings, there it was: the smooth threads of her pink scarf, with paisleys looping back and forth across the material. She hadn't forgotten the lessons of the paisleys and what was contained in them. Sensible lessons: keep good thoughts, do good deeds, and tell the truth.

She tucked everything back in the drawers and closed them, throwing the scarf over the back of her chair. She had heard that the last few months of pregnancy were filled with worries and the drive to make a nest. Well, any nest of hers might be pretty disorganized and messy, but colorful and filled with lessons. She sat massaging her belly, amazed at how this big round ball could belong to her body.

Chapter 18
Ravens' Nest

Sean pulled a dark blue bandanna from his jeans to wipe sweat from his eyes. *It's going to be a scorcher today,* he thought. Sean knew the desert could easily get into the triple digits, but usually, it was later on in the summer. But, with all the unpredictability now, it could get very hot today. Here he was back in the dry desert air, back trying to solve the mystery of the naked blond, Erin.

He'd had a great week of surfing, waves that held up, the water's temperature on the cold side, just how he liked it. He'd seen a lot more of MaeAnn. He smiled thinking about her and how they were a couple now since they had agreed to see only each other. Still, she hadn't come into his bed and she hadn't invited him into hers, but he knew her body enough to know it would be beautiful when that happened, and he was confident that it would happen soon.

He'd made a date to go surfing with her. She'd tried surfing, she'd told him, but couldn't stand up without sinking the tip of the board and being flung into the water. She was "pearling," and he'd told her he would work with her until she could ride all the way in.

And that woman with the scarf he'd seen in San Francisco, he wished he'd asked her more, but then the man had came along, someone who looked so familiar, Pakistani or Iraqi. Sean thought. The man walked by, and he'd looked back briefly with a frown, or was it a scowl? Sean simply put his hand up to wave again, but the man didn't reply; he just abruptly turned away and walked on with the red-headed woman.

Sean was sure he'd remember the place he'd buried the paisley scarf, but even though he'd checked the map he'd made, when he hiked in the heat to the spot below the petroglyph rocks and dug just where he thought he'd buried it, no luck. He checked the picture he had taken; yes, this was definitely the spot. He wiped his dirt-clogged hands with the bandanna. He'd dug all around and couldn't see any signs of the scarf with silver-edged paisleys scattered across it. Damn, now what?

As he turned to go, a large jack rabbit crossed in front of him. It leapt away up the hill. He recalled his vision from before, and suddenly was on high alert. As he watched the rabbit's zig zagging run he saw pieces of cardboard scattered around. Someone, or something, maybe coyotes, had dug up the box. Sean knew the wild dogs to be pretty curious and have good sniffers for human scent.

He walked over to where the cardboard scraps were strewn in the sandy dirt when a shiny raven flew close to him squawking. The bird dove at him again. When he followed the raven's flight he saw shreds of pink hanging from the sage brush. And up on the branches of an incense cedar there was a second raven with a strip hanging from her beak. Building a nest, and this was already a beauty, pink wool pieces tucked into the mesquite, into sticks of willow, into dry grasses, cypress, and small twigs of cottonwood trees.

He'd always admired the ability of birds to build, weave really, he thought, much like his tribe wove their baskets. He laughed as the large birds flew close to him again. To think this scarf, just like the ones he'd seen in Afghanistan, in Pakistan, had ended up here in the California desert was just too much. He chuckled again at the absurdities of life. His contraband, now tucked into a ravens' nest, soon to hold eggs which would hatch, be fed, then fledge the nest. Kind of late for nest building, Sean thought, but often ravens hatched chicks into June.

Well, so much for the idea of contacting Erin with the lure of a scarf. He'd have to think of something else. He wasn't sure why he needed to see her again. Of course, she was pretty enough, and he couldn't help looking her over before he'd covered her up with his jacket as he'd waited for the ambulance to come. But he had MaeAnn now, with her warm tones and dark black hair, some red showing through where the beach weather had bleached it.

What had caused those marks on Erin's wrists? He desperately wanted to be sure that Erin was all right. He'd seen so much death, and this time, death was beaten—and he'd been a part of it, of something good for a change.

He took out his camera and clicked several pictures of the nest and the ravens before both birds set up a screeching warning, and started croaking and gargling at him. One, probably the male, started to dive at him. Protecting their nest, he thought. Birds, more monogamous than most humans, ducking and waving his arms at the bird. He picked up one short skinny piece of paisley and tucked it into his pocket.

He'd been having success lately selling his photos. One gallery owner told him he had "a good eye for composition." He thought today's pictures might be a really good. The pictures of the wolves, the ones of birds and coyotes... those were ones that always sold. People needed to reconnect with nature, he thought, as he hiked back down the hill, sweating as he went, and this time just letting the sweat drip, stinging his eyes with its salt. He was a little dizzy today. Sometimes his injuries could affect him like that. Nothing to worry about, though. At his last VA medical exam. He'd been told he was doing well.

He slowly finished walking back down the path to his motorcycle and tossed everything into his saddlebag, including a small remnant of the pink scarf he'd picked up. He hoped he could still use it to prove to Erin that he had been the one who'd found her.

As soon as he got cell connection, he stopped on the side of the road to call MaeAnn.

"Come over tomorrow. I will show you how to balance on a board at my place, and then if the waves are good, we can surf together. I'll stay with you until you are standing tall and riding in."

"Sean, I work in the morning, of course, but I could come over after that."

104

"The waves won't be as good then, but off-shore breezes will come up, and that might help the waves hold their shape. Why don't I meet you at the cafe and I can walk you over to my place?"

MaeAnn hesitated for a second, but then he could hear her let out a breath, "Okay, that sounds good," she said. Sean was elated; this was the first time she had agreed to come over.

As he started his motorcycle again, he felt the stirrings of the Santa Anas. In California, the winds were a bonus for the surfers, but were also the cause of wind-driven wildfires. The state was plagued now with fires and floods. Still, he loved the place and didn't ever plan to leave.

When she was coherent, his bio mom had a lot of interesting ideas to share. The main idea was that everything was alive, the rocks, the sand, everything. Sean grew up with that idea, and he still believed it. She was the one who told him that his ancestors had made these petroglyphs.

Could the people who'd painted these rocks, who created these petroglyphs, his own people, understand the power of nature better than we could now? He always loved the Mesa Verde cliff dwellings—the Pueblos Indians, masterful rock masons, had carved out their houses. People back then, when they had to be aware of volcanic activity, tidal waves, winds that could bring down trees onto their shelter.

As he rode along, he thought about the mustard and wild radish and how tall it had grown this year. Finally rains had come and everyone in the state was celebrating this relief from drought.

He was celebrating too, what seemed to him a change in his life with success with his art, his new girlfriend. Life is good, he thought gunning his bike to get to the coast a little faster.

105

Chapter 19
Splashed

Elizabeth's cell phone rang, and when she looked, she saw it was Maria. Maria, oh, how she'd missed Maria since giving up graduate school. Her friend was continuing on in Marine Biology, while Elizabeth was growing bigger every day, being pummeled from the inside by her baby boy. This was something she and Maria didn't share.

"Maria, hello friend, you must have just gotten back from Mexico. How was it?"

"The baby whales are born; the calves are launched. It was beautiful to watch. I traveled back and forth between Magdalene Bay and the Sea of Cortes. I'm still high from it all. You know I'm in love with dolphins and whales, but after watching this for three months, I want to focus on whales, blue, gray or humpback.

"Well then, you might like me right now; I'm as big as a whale."

"Oh, that's right, how could I forget the baby—little Babar, right?"

"Something like that," Elizabeth answered laughing. *Bahar was not an easy name to remember,* she thought.

"Well, I would love to see you in your whale goddess shape, but I also want to see real whales. I just heard on the local news that the San Francisco Bay is filled right now with humpbacks. A huge number, very unusual," Maria explained. "Come join me on the bay, you know where.....Embarcadero pier 30. Can you? "

Elizabeth could never refuse Maria, ever since they'd met over a meal of greasy calamari in the student lounge at college. She was from Salvador and was persistent, taking honors in most of her classes, and urging Elizabeth not to drop out of her art history program. Normally Maria's powers of persuasion would have worked on Elizabeth, but she couldn't take another day of studying Sanskrit and writing endless papers. Where would it ever lead her anyway? No, she had to take a break. "Yes, I can, and I will, " answered Elizabeth.

An hour later, Elizabeth was on a bus to the Embarcadero to meet Maria and whale watch. She brought her water bottle and a couple of oranges, but she knew that Maria would want a real meal after whale watching. She'd want fish—fresh "catch of the day." Elizabeth always found this odd for someone who loved the ocean and all its creatures, how much her friend loved the taste of fish.

"Anchovies, millions of them coming in on the tide, is what the whales are after," Maria said as they walked out to the end of the pier, where a small crowd had gathered. The excitement, the expectations ratcheted up after a tall thin woman in shorts and a French striped T-shirt shouted out, "Over there!" Everyone turned left to see where she pointed. A huge body came out of the water, flipper first, followed by a splashy loud bang of its tail on the water. The whales were breaching, and she and Maria and the crowd were in for a great show.

"Geez, Maria, did you see how close he came to that boat and its mooring?"

"Yes, that's what they're afraid of, the boats, the traffic across the bay, the disorientation of the underwater sounds. They don't want another Humphrey, if you remember that poor guy who ended up in the Sacramento River and then, unbelievably, in a slough."

"What I remember about Humphrey is that the Navy helped lure him back to San Francisco Bay and then the ocean by playing recorded whale sounds, and it worked. "

"They probably felt guilty for all those sonic booms they do underwater that mess with the whales, so they had to do something that made themselves look good!" Maria said. Elizabeth smiled at her. She knew Maria was fierce about the whales. Maria felt it her personal mission to protect them.

The whale, or was it another one, breached, and a communal "Ohhhhh" went up from the crowd. This was exciting. The size of these sea creatures so close, and not where they would normally be, suddenly made Elizabeth reach over to "high five" Maria. She felt exhilarated and alive and happy to be standing here watching the bay for another whale.

"Great sights; this is such fun Maria, thanks for calling me."

"Well, I'm surprised you could board a bus with that big belly you've got now," Maria said playfully, reaching over to pat her tummy.

"The people on the bus were very polite; they were saying, 'move aside, move aside,' and well, yes, laughing at me as well. But not in a mean way."

"You have almost reached that hallowed status: Motherhood."

"But as I understand, it doesn't mean Sainthood. Yipes, I can't really imagine being called *Mommy* or even *Mother,* much less holding a baby in the middle of the night. I've been reading every book I can find on preparing for birth, on how to breastfeed, on what supplies I'll need, and even about post-partum depression and how many months after giving birth before I'll get my periods back. Everything. There is too much information and not enough information all at the same time." Elizabeth looked over at Maria who was still focused on the whales.

"And Najid has been traveling a lot, so he hasn't been around to give me sympathy and to cuddle me. He seems one of those unusual guys who likes to see a pregnant woman's body."

"Sounds like you're overwhelmed, my friend, but someone calling you *Mommy,* I can easily imagine it. I'd like it myself, but it doesn't look like it will ever happen for me And *Daddy,* well, he's got the right idea to appreciate your new figure. And how to be a mother, it will probably just come to you, but I know you like

108

to analyze things. Honey, just get ready for a big change!" Maria said, looking intently at the bay waters for another whale.

"You can't believe how much my life has changed in the period of eight months! I can't believe it myself." Maria turned to smile at Elizabeth, nodded her head, and then dug her binoculars from her backpack to scan the bay.

Elizabeth felt a sudden dampening and looked around to see if someone had splashed her with water or if a whale had jumped close by, but nothing. And now a gush of water poured down the insides of her legs and wet her leggings, leaving a small puddle at her feet. She was shocked. Her strappy red sandals completely soaked.

Without meaning to, Elizabeth groaned and said, "What the hell...?" Maria put the binoculars down and followed her friend's eyes to her feet. Just then. Elizabeth felt a wave of pain ripple across her belly that made her double over and grab onto her friend's arm.

"Oh, honey, I think your water just broke," Maria said.

The woman next to them who'd spotted that first whale looked at Elizabeth and said, "I'm calling an ambulance."

"No, please, I'll just go home," Elizabeth said just before another stab in her abdomen had her slumping to the ground. This time more water, but tinged with blood, pooled by her feet.

"How did you get here?" the woman asked.

"She rode the bus; I'm parked by the Ferry Building," Maria said, "I could go get my car, but I don't want to leave my friend here alone."

"I'm Janis, and I'll stay with her. What's your name anyway?" she asked, looking down at Elizabeth, who didn't answer. "She's Elizabeth, and I'm Maria. I will text you my phone number. Thank you." Maria turned away and broke into a run.

"And if it seems necessary, I'll call for an ambulance," Janis yelled after Maria.

The crowd had stepped back and away from Elizabeth.

"Now, don't worry, Elizabeth. I'm going to stay here with you, and you will be fine," Janis said.

Elizabeth felt a mix of emotions, first embarrassment, then confusion, and finally, downright fear. Could it really be that she was going into labor? This was three weeks earlier than she'd planned for, and she realized she was not at all ready. Yes, she had a few clothes; she had been given a few things by neighbors and her scattering of friends, but what she wasn't ready for was the labor itself. And, there was Najid to consider.

"Oh Maria, no, don't leave me here," Elizabeth shouted after her friend.

"It's all right honey, I'll be right back," she called out behind her the words drifting off along the waterfront. *Maria was fast, a sprinter in college. She really means it,* Elizabeth thought.

"Okay," Janis said, "I have Maria's phone number, and I'll call her if there is any change or if I have to call for an ambulance." Janis was kneeling by Elizabeth when a man in the crowd stepped over with a small blanket which he threw down across the pier planks, and then he helped Janis move Elizabeth over onto it.

"Maybe this will be a little more comfortable," he said as he sat down next to the two women.

"No, I'm all wet, I don't want to get this blanket all messed up!" Elizabeth said, frantic and trying to pull the blanket out from under her.

The man laughed, "My kids have spilled a million gallons of lemonade on the blanket over the years. It washes! Anyway, I'm a fireman, and I have seen births, and it looks to me like you're going into labor."

"No, I'm not!" Elizabeth said, holding her side. "I just can't be." The fireman didn't say anything more but stayed seated by her.

"So is there someone I need to call, or you need to call, maybe your husband or family?" Janis asked.

"I've got to get in touch with Najid, but I really don't know what this water breaking means since I'm not due for another three weeks. And anyway, no husband, he's just a father, this baby's father that is." Stammering meant Elizabeth was very anxious. And why shouldn't she be? *This was foreign terrain,* Elizabeth thought. She smiled at Janis, and shrugged her shoulders. She wasn't sure why, maybe in a kind of apologetic gesture. Then again, the pain. And again.

"He's still the father, so he should know what's happening," Janis said in a way that meant there was no room for argument. Just then, another whale leapt up into the air and splashed back down, sending a shower of water into the crowd. *At least I'm not the only wet one,* Elizabeth thought as she watched people turn their attention back to the bay and to their wet clothes. They were laughing, and so she started to laugh too. She really didn't know what was so funny, but she kept laughing until Janis said,

"Elizabeth, the call we need to make."

"Here, take my cell," Elizabeth said, reaching into her jacket pocket. Handing Janis her phone, she said, "His name is Najid. But I just can't talk to him about this."

"Oh, that's a different name—but a nice name," Janis said.

"Persian," Elizabeth said. Thinking of how he'd gifted her with Rumi and lilies and now, this baby that he'd been stroking recently through the tight skin of her belly.

"Okay then, I'll ring his cell and hand the phone back to you so you can talk to him." Elizabeth now noticed that Janis spoke with a British accent.

"No, I said I can't talk," Elizabeth was panting through more pain, "I can't talk right now. Just tell him I'll call later when I, when I," she said through deep breaths, "when I know more."

"Don't worry—what's your name again?"

"Elizabeth."

"Don't worry, Elizabeth; his phone is ringing right now, and I'll just tell him the basics."

"He's had a kid before," Elizabeth said. She wasn't really sure why she said it since that child was gone. And the child's mother, too, Najid's wife. Both gone. Elizabeth started to cry.

"So he's an experienced guy, that's good," Janis answered. "Don't worry, he'll know what all this means."

"I wish I did," Elizabeth said dabbing at her eyes. The next thing she remembered was the sharply pitched sound of an ambulance siren and the bumping noises the tires of the gurney made as she was rolled her across the pier. And then the buzz of her vibrating cell phone in her pants pocket.

"You passed out, honey, but I'm right here with you. I'll follow the ambulance to the hospital." Maria shouted into the ambulance as the EMTs were reaching to shut the doors.

"Maria, I'm so scared. What should I do?"

"Breathe, friend—breathe and nature will take care of you. I've seen it, and I know you're going to be fine." The ambulance door was slammed shut, and the wail of the siren started up again, so loud Elizabeth put her hands over her ears. The big guy next to her gently took her hands away and put them on her belly as he placed an oxygen mask over her mouth and nose. Funny, but she felt she was being rocked in a cradle.

She barely felt or heard the vibrations in her pocket; for once, the cell phone didn't seem important, even if it might be the father of this baby. All she could do was concentrate, like Maria had told her, on breathing and on finding a rhythm of a song that would match the pulsing sensations that had taken over her body. She knew she was no longer in control. She tried to push at the oxygen mask until she realized she could not move her hands. She had been strapped in.

She started to sing a lullaby her mother had always sung to her and her sister, "Hush little baby, don't say a word, papa's gonna buy you a mockingbird, and if that mockingbird don't sing, papa's gonna buy you a diamond ring."

But the EMT said, "Just sing the song in your head. We'll be at the hospital very, very soon." And then she thought she heard him sing the words, "Hush little baby don't you cry… Daddy loves you, and so do I…" And then, nothing.

Chapter 20
Escape

"I'm in Palmdale at a hospital; the phone says room 22. Come pick me up. Don't say much to the desk; the police are watching out for me. You'll have to be sneaky."

"You know me, Deirdre, I can do that. And I owe you one for the last time you helped me."

Deirdre was still struggling with headaches. What she remembered of the hospital was the intense need to leave and then waking to her cousin Martha's blond hair brushing her face as she tried to get Deirdre to cooperate. "Move your legs to the edge; sit up! You said you wanted to get out. Now come on, up, up."

Deirdre slowly moved over to the edge of the bed and sat up. The room whirled around for a minute, and then she had to put her head in her hands and keep herself from vomiting. "Stand now," Martha ordered. *She was used to bossing old people around,* Deirdre thought.

So she stood, and Martha wrapped her in a muumuu-like dress. Deirdre slipped into some flip-flops, and they walked as fast as possible out the back door to Martha's car. The rest Deirdre could barely recall. Just driving and driving and driving. That's all.

Deirdre was in worse shape than she thought. Muscles on fire, headache, nausea. Opioids. She was able to make out the word "naloxone" on one of the IV bags as she was leaving her room. Bastards! And she didn't even know which bastards to blame. Just that in the desert, she had caught on fire.

Chapter 21
Journey into Motherhood

"My phone, my phone... got to answer it," Elizabeth's arms were bound to her sides. She couldn't move, and she started screaming. "Please, answer my cell." Elizabeth looked intently at the EMT. Even with the oxygen mask on, he had heard her.

The big man with a wide smile fished the phone out of Elizabeth's pocket and answered it.

"Hello, Elizabeth is unable to answer right now; who is calling, please? Okay... okay, she thought it might be you." The man said quietly to Elizabeth, "It is someone who says he's your husband. I will have to hold this to your ear, miss. We have you strapped in."

"Husband? I don't have a... Oh. It's Najid, thank God," she said, trying to reach for the phone again and panicking for a minute when she forgot that her arms were tied down to her sides.

"I will have to take this oxygen mask off, so make it quick," the EMT said to her in what she thought sounded like a Jamaican accent.

"Well, I don't know what to tell him—*ohhhhhh*," she groaned as she felt another sharp pain in her belly.

"Do you want me to tell him where we are taking you?"

"Yes, please, yes." With that, Elizabeth closed her eyes, and when she opened them, the interior of the ambulance started to spin.

*I'm going to pass out, s*he thought.

At that moment the EMT clamped the oxygen mask over her face, but when he looked down at Elizabeth, she wasn't responding to the oxygen yet.

"Turn on the speed," he yelled to the driver. He shouted the name of the hospital into her cell phone and dropped it back down onto her chest. She felt it fall, but somehow she felt a sparrow had landed on her while she was sitting in her garden.

******

All the babies in the world and all their mothers went through this? Elizabeth heard a strange sound and it took a minute to realize it was her own voice. She was screaming and swearing and panting so hard she couldn't really get a breath. The male nurse next to her put his hand on her shoulder. "Breathe—slow down and breathe with me."

Like another person's voice echoing in the room, she heard herself say, "*Don't you touch me. Get... away!*"

The room was spinning, and everything receded. A woman dressed in scrubs leaned close to her to say quietly:

"Listen, Elizabeth. I'm your delivery Dr., and I'm going to give you something for the pain. Your baby is stressed; we may have to do a C-section."

Baby. That's right; this was all about her and Najid's little baby, the one who had planted himself like a watermelon seed she had swallowed, which had changed her body until she didn't recognize herself with the big round breasts and the full, taut belly. Right now all she could think of was herself, pain knocking any rosy baby thoughts aside. She felt like she was in a fierce battle with her own body, and she wasn't sure who was winning. The nurses suddenly pushed her over on her side, and she felt a sharp stab of a needle.

"Don't worry, you'll feel better very soon. But we may have to take this baby out—or if not, we may be helping you a lot with the delivery."

"Help me," Elizabeth shouted, "No C-section. Where's Dr. Chong?"

Elizabeth went back to counting between contractions now that the pain had slacked off. When is this baby coming? This was a different kind of marathon; she was not on top of it in the same way she always tried to be in control of everything.

"We are going to try to turn the baby slightly; he is coming shoulder first and that is causing the pain. You shouldn't feel too much," he said as she saw his arm disappear under the sheets beyond her knees. Someone else pushed down on her belly. She thought of her bike rides again, pedaling and pedaling, breathing and seeing miles of bay go by....once again, she felt like air. Nothing hurt now; and soon she closed her eyes. The last thing she remembered seeing was the nurse's name tag: Steve.

"Stay with us here Elizabeth, we need your help!" The Dr. was back with three nurses.

"Elizabeth; concentrate with me. We're going to give you more oxygen and we are transferring you to another gurney in case we need to get the baby out in a hurry. You will need to help us by lifting up a bit."

Elizabeth tried to move but felt paralyzed. "I just can't," she told the Dr..

Nurse Steve came over and turned Elizabeth on her other side. She noticed that now she felt different; she couldn't say how, but the freight train had reached its destination. Then a ragged feeling, and she groaned with all her might and pushed down.

"Good, the baby's in position, and she's pushing," Steve said to the young nurse. "Too late for a section now."

Her womb had worked after all, she thought, not only to cocoon her baby but now to expel him. Her little boy. Where was the father in all this? Where was Najid?

She called out his name, "Najiiiiddd...."

The nurses looked at one another.

Then a man, dark with a green mask covering his mouth came over quickly and grabbed her hand.

"I'm here, Elizabeth."

Oh, Najid. He's here. Elizabeth stared up at him.

"I've been here for a while, but they told me to leave the room until you were almost ready for the birth. Here I am." As she looked up at him she could barely think of them together, reading Rumi out on her patio, or walking together across town for dinner.

116

And now such intimacy with all these strangers and with him. She closed her eyes and squeezed Najid's hand tightly as she pushed down again; the nurse squeezed down on her belly. White lilies, and their fragrance came forward, an image from the back of her mind.

"The baby is crowning, Elizabeth. We can see his head," Steve said.

"It's a boy. That's right, my son," Najid shouted out, "Our baby, Elizabeth and you are doing great!"

Another contraction and the nurses pushed her upright into a nearly sitting position shoving pillows behind her. "One more and the baby will be out," Steve said. She wondered for a second how Najid felt about this other man being in the room with her legs spread and everything about her womanhood exposed. The thoughts she was having seemed random and disconnected from what she was going through.

A cry erupted from down below. The baby. He was being pulled out and immediately wailed away. *That means he can breathe,* she thought. Najid was kissing her cheeks where the tears oozed out. She hadn't even known she was crying.

"Our boy," he said And then, when she looked at his eyes, she could see they were clouded with tears of his own. "Our baby has come!" he yelled out again, *as though he were announcing it to the whole staff, to the whole world,* she thought. In spite of herself, Elizabeth smiled. The baby was put on her belly. She looked him over, head of dark hair, arms waving in the air, wailing away at his arrival on planet Earth. She put a finger on his head of hair, still damp, and she thought. This is it. I have joined all the billions of others. I am a mother, and you, little guy, will have to put up with me.

Chapter 22
Picturing a Future

Before he'd even unpacked, Sean got out his camera and plugged it into his laptop. He thought he'd gotten some very good pictures. There were pictures of the raven's nest, pink paisleys barely visible, except to him. Most people would just see strips of pink wound into the nest. And, of course, they wouldn't know what it meant to him. No one would know about that day in the desert. Erin, lying on the side of the road.

He paused to look at one shot. It was excellent; he had captured the male leaving the nest, wings spread wide and his head and curved beak visible. He had shot the nest closer in, the shiny parts of the scarf glittering in the desert sun. It was just the kind of dramatic shot that made him happy. Probably this one would make his gallery happy too. They had sold many pictures Sean had taken out in the desert. It was clearly a winner. He pounded his fist on his table and shouted, "Yes!"

He clicked through the rest of his pictures, stopping to look carefully at one of the petroglyph, with a close up of multiple scratchings: a bear's paw, a goat, stars, the figure of a person. More than graffiti of the past, these were humans trying to say something, artists trying to leave their mark for others to see. He felt a little like that with the photographs he made. He knew collectors had them in their fancy houses, and that was okay with him. Someone would know he had frozen something in time. He straightened out a few things in the petroglyph picture, cropped it and attached it to his message for his Palm Springs dealer. He had already attached the raven with the nest in the background.

He went on to crop and size a couple of images from the train trip, a particularly nice one of mustard and one of a cotton field with a wrecked Ford truck from the 30s. He would think about which gallery might accept these.

He also mailed the nest and mustard images to the local coast gallery.

What do you think? I see this as printed on metal.
Sean.

Before he unplugged his laptop, he scrolled back to pictures to post into his MaeAnn folder.

He smiled at the one she had asked a stranger to take of her with Sean at the beach. They were smiling at each other. He guessed they just couldn't hide the way they felt about each other. Well, for sure, the way he felt about her. Later today he'd see her. She'd be here for the first time, and he'd be helping her become a real surfer.

He had an idea about how to get her to balance correctly. She didn't seem to be afraid of the water at all, and she was strong; he'd seen that. Her arms were taut and brown. He thought that lifting dishes in a café for years had made her fit.

She was energetic, and he found it contagious. Like he could be a kid again turning cartwheels and doing flips with Abby and his foster brother Rick. He'd found out that as long as he picked up physical things quickly, no one would tease him in school about how slowly he read or how much time it took him to calculate numbers to solve math problems. He felt so comfortable with MaeAnn. He would help her today and it would bring them even closer.

His phone buzzed. A message from the Palm Springs Gallery. *How soon can we get these, Sean? We would like to have multiples and in different sizes. If you need financing for that, let us know. Love the images, Mark.*

Good, they would pay for the cost of producing the prints. Phew. They'd been good to him, but he knew it was because his work sold.

Sean got up and rubbed his ribs, his leg, the usual places that hurt. Especially on a day like today when the fog was in. Something about damp weather bothered him more.

He would sit down later and search the internet again in an attempt to locate Erin. She seemed to have slipped out of sight, and with good reason. He hoped she was safe from the bastards that tried to kill her. He pushed his chair back because right now he just wanted to get himself and his little apartment cleaned up for MaeAnn.

He made himself a cup of coffee and then took out the remnants of a doughnut he had picked up before his ride home. It was a little stale, but that didn't matter as he dipped it in his coffee and imagined what MaeAnn would think when he showed her the picture of the raven on his laptop with its nest of Pink Paisley. He thought she would be impressed. He was impressed himself, and it didn't seem real yet: success with his photography, and a girlfriend like MaeAnn.

Life certainly was beautiful today.

Chapter 23
Bundle

She was grabbed by another sharp pain."What now? I thought I was through!" Elizabeth was astonished that there was still more to do. The baby was here; she'd seen his little red face, his mass of dark hair.

"Placenta, one more push, and it's out," the nurse said.

With all her might, Elizabeth pushed, and the placenta slid out. She'd forgotten about this part, even though she'd read all about it.

"Congratulations, that is the last push you're going to need; the *Tree of Life* has been expelled," said the guy in scrubs as he reached toward her and she felt a swoosh of air down at her cervix. She realized it was the placenta being whisked away. Cats eat theirs, but she had no need to even see this Tree of Life. All she could do was stay on the bed, on the earth. She had a dull humming in her ears, and the room was gently rocking. Was San Francisco having an earthquake? She thought she might throw up, but instead, she closed her eyes and saw the multiple images of Najid's hand in hers.

"Blood, here, she's got to be transfused," she heard but couldn't respond. She didn't even realize she was not expected to say or do anything but lie there.

"I'll do a match," said someone else." All she could feel was Najid squeezing her hand tighter and tighter. He said something in Farsi: *man kheili khoshhalam.*

It was something he'd said a lot to her lately when he'd patted her big belly. He told her it meant: "I am very happy." And then Najid cried out, "Allllaahhhhh!" A nurse came running over and hung a bag of red just above Elizabeth's head. Another nurse fussed with her IV, and then Najid again, "Alllllaaaahhhh", the last thing she remembered.

******

A tiny wrapped bundle was handed to Elizabeth, but she felt so weak she could hardly hold her son. And her eyes kept closing. She forced herself awake so she could finally take a good look at this little boy. She was just uncovering the baby's tiny feet when Najid reached across her belly and took the baby.

"Elizabeth, you need rest. You are still weak from giving birth." Najid said to her.

He kissed her forehead and then kissed the baby's. He looked intently down at the bundle in his arms and then looked across at Elizabeth.

"So, what shall we call him my sweet dear? Omid, Bahar, Rashid, Akbar?"

"You know I just can't think about this right now, Najid. I am just going to call him Son, for right now, okay?"

"Okay, Elizabeth, we have time. A name is important; it sets you into the world with a mission to fulfill."

"I never thought about a name like that, as a task to be done," Elizabeth answered wearily, "but I see you have a point."

On top of everything else, she was now responsible for someone's mission in life, all because of the choice of a name. Elizabeth felt overwhelmed. Her breasts were hurting, and now her abdominal area felt so strange; when she put her hand on her belly, there was no round bump, just a lump of doughy feeling flesh. There was the occasional small contraction, what she knew to be the uterus trying to get back down to normal.

Just then, the baby started to cry, fussing really, not a big cry. *Kind of polite,* she thought.

Nurse Steve came over and plucked the baby out of Najid's arms. Najid looked startled to have the baby taken and started to reach out, but the nurse placed her son on Elizabeth's chest.

"He needs to start sucking so that your milk will come in good. I'm going to have a lactation specialist come in to get you started. We won't have you do it for long right now; you're still

122

weak and getting blood. The baby must be able to breastfeed, or take a bottle before we can release him from the hospital."

Elizabeth put a finger through a curl of Son's hair and sighed.

"What is it?" Najid asked

"Oh, I don't know. I didn't even expect those sounds to come out of me. Like so much of this, it seems I'm not in control of myself at all. I guess the word "blood" got me. There is so much of it involved with birth," The new mother started to cry. Najid wasn't quite sure what to do.

Najid said, "Don't worry, you are going to be a great mother. You are going to learn everything that you need to know, and I will be there for you, for our son, whenever you need me. Believe me, Elizabeth. This is going to bring you so much happiness. Our boy will be a blessing to us both."

"You're right," she said, "I'm not really feeling sad, just that I can't believe I'm a mother and my breasts are filled with milk and soon at home in my flat I'll be rocking a baby.

I wish my mother were still alive. I wish I knew how to reach my sister to tell her this amazing news about the baby, about me, about us having a son. That's why I'm crying, Najid." Elizabeth pulled out a Kleenex from the box the hospital had just given her and dabbed at her eyes.

He shook his head; "Yes,"Najid said, "I understand that you are nervous about this new life you will be leading." Najid said, "I have been here before, I am good with babies. I can help with our son. " Elizabeth thought about him, his wife and his little daughter gone forever, and then that realization made her cry even harder until Najid put his lips to hers and kissed her sounds away.

"Son" nestled into her breasts, not really interested in nursing, he fell asleep, and for that she was so grateful. She didn't feel she could give anything more right now; it was enough just to smell the new smells of her own son and to fall in love with this little bundle that belonged to her. The bundle with no real name yet, but two parents who welcomed him into this land of light and dark, love and despair, and all that the world has to offer.

Chapter 24
Little Bahar

The scary time of blood and the baby's coming early, and everything else was over. Finally, his son had learned to drink from Elizabeth's breasts, and she had regained her strength.

Najid found Elizabeth to be so different from Zara. His wife had been a woman who showed off in her pregnancy. Zara had been ecstatic with her round belly, with her easy birth, and happy and calm taking their daughter home. Elizabeth seemed astonished by everything to do with being a mother, her belly, the birth and now, even the child himself. It seemed too much for her. He felt a strong affection for her, but he wondered if he could ever love anyone the way he had loved his daughter and Zara.

"You will settle into a time schedule, and your breasts will only let out milk when the baby needs to eat." The lactation specialist was demonstrating a nursing bra, with flaps that come down and pads to soak up excess milk.

"Oh, okay," Elisabeth nodded. She wondered at the size of her breasts, so big, and she'd always been happy to have small breasts. Filled with milk, just like a goat or a cow. But part of her was proud of her body for cooperating and providing something her baby needed.

Najid stood in the corner holding the yet-to-be-named baby. He began kissing his son's forehead while she hobbled about the hospital room, her home for a week while she gained back strength, and until the baby was able to really take her breast milk efficiently. There was a lot she had learned about birthing and the rhythm of an infant's life, and now there was so much more to learn. Suddenly she stopped packing and turned to Najid: "I'm afraid."

"What are you afraid of?" he asked.

"Well, just about everything...all it takes to be a mother, a parent. This is a forever thing, and I've always avoided forevers." She blinked back tears.

Najid came over and placed the baby in her arms.

"Look at him. He is perfect, and he is ours. He is not afraid." Najid hoped Elizabeth did not see the tears in his eyes.

"The Dr. says all the crying I've done here, it's not from pain from the stitches or from the milk coming in, but from depression and that it's common."

"Depression? No! You should feel great joy my dear. Look at what you have created. What we've created." As he said this, he took the baby back, and she returned to picking up and packing up everything in the room to take home. She picked up the flowers and looked toward Najid. "Leave them for the nurses," he said. She bundled up the few clothes that Maria had thought to bring in for the baby, preemie size. Najid had gotten to meet Maria then, and they liked each other right away.

Najid and Elizabeth had been taught how to wrap a diaper with the padding in the front, and how to duck when they were not quick enough with the diaper.

So many Dr.s, nurses, and specialists had seen Elizabeth and his son; this is not how it had been with his little daughter's birth. That had all been so simple.

"Okay," she said, "let's get out of here."

As they approached the doorway, Najid fell to his knees, the baby in his arms. "Thank you, Elizabeth, thank you for our son." He was choked up, and then she remembered his loss.

Oh, dear God, she thought. *I hadn't even considered how hard this was on him too.*

"Najid, I'm so sorry. I haven't forgotten that our son had a sister once. My heart hurts for you. Now I understand how someone can feel about their baby. I really know now what you must have gone through. Oh, a child dying, it's too much to bear."

A nurse came and insisted on wheeling Elizabeth out. Najid tried to insist that he should be the one to do this, but this

126

nurse was more insistent, so Elizabeth sat in the wheelchair with a bag of her clothes, everything the hospital had given her piled on her lap. A bunch of papers in a big envelope and her purse stuck out of her over-filled backpack. She couldn't understand why she wasn't allowed to walk out on her own, and neither could he. *After all*, Najid thought, *she is not an invalid, just a normal new mother.*

At the bottom of the ramp, the nurse told Najid to get the car and that the baby would have to have a car seat or the hospital would not release him.

Najid had rented a car, a little blue Prius. The infant seat was in place, and he'd only had a little trouble getting it into the car.

Outside the hospital, Najid took in a deep breath of the salty air. Today was a brilliant day, no fog, and he could see clear across the bay. Small sailboats were dots in the water. The Golden Gate Bridge stood red and bold. It felt so good to be outside of hospital walls and to leave behind all the sounds of the hospital, the constant babble and interruption.

"I am so glad to be going home, Najid. I just hope I can remember all I was taught about being a mother to a newborn!"

"Don't worry, I can help you, and any time you need me, call me up, even if it's in the middle of the night. I will be right over." Najid worried. He had to believe it would all go well.

A couple came along, and were about to walk up the hospital steps when they stopped first and said, "Oh, a newborn, congratulations. Is this your first?" the fair-skinned woman asked. Elizabeth looked at Najid, and he just nodded yes. They exchanged a look that said it all. *Her first, not his.* The woman said, "Can I see him, or is it a her?"

Najid was just about to set the baby in the car and strap him in. But he swung the baby up so the woman could see him clearly.

"A boy," Najid said

"Adorable. Such a lot of dark hair. He will be a handsome boy." she added.

"Bahar," Elizabeth whispered. And then, looking at Najid and then at the couple, she said, "Thank you, his name is Bahar."

Najid smiled and nodded, "Yes, our little Bahar. In Persian, it means springtime."

The couple looked at each other, and then the woman said, "Oh, that's a nice name, very unusual and in the nick of time, just before the Spring Equinox."

"Don't worry," said the tall African American man, "He'll get used to it." And he laughed a big deep laugh that soon had all of them laughing.

This son, with his tiny penis, little testicles, presented a whole different baby look from what Najid had experienced before. This was all new to him, and yet he welcomed the chance to start again as a father. He felt a strong pull to be with Elizabeth forever if there were such a thing. He wanted to have a family, a wife, this child. He let out a big sigh, which made Elizabeth turn to look at him.

Najid put the last bag into the back of the car and then hooked Bahar into the new car seat, more like a recliner for the little boy, he thought. With Zara, she had refused to give up her baby to a car seat and insisted on carrying the baby in her arms on the short ride home from the hospital in Tehran. Here, that would mean a ticket. And he had been told, it would be very dangerous for the child.

Elizabeth took his hand, "Nej, thank you for being at my side the whole time."

Najid was tempted to quote a poem, but resisted. "Of course, you are my sweet, and this is our amazing Son. Let's get you home now." He drove away, the sun shining through the window and onto Elizabeth. He looked over at her, and she gave him a quick smile.

Yes, he thought. *This moment will do.*

Chapter 25
In the Boat Painted Blue

Being a mother was so much more than she had ever imagined or learned from the new baby book she'd barely finished before the whales and the splashing and the dash to the hospital. The fact that Najid had quickly come and that he'd found her was another small miracle.

When she was sure Bahar was getting milk, gulping it down, which meant a lot of back-patting for the baby after, she opened The Persian Poets book and turned to Rumi:

> *Late, by myself, in the boat of myself,*
> *no light and no land anywhere,*
> *cloud cover thick. I try to stay*
> *just above the surface,*
> *yet I'm already under*
> *and living with the ocean.*

Elizabeth sat up straighter and started to pat her son's back and then rock him back and forth to get him to sleep. He was fussing and rubbing his face back and forth, seeking her nipple. She was so tired. She put him down on the bed and looked at him while he squalled, his cheeks turning red with what seemed like fury. She decided to check his diaper. *Oh that's it, he's wet and he probably needs to poop, even though that wasn't happening much yet,* she thought. He was three weeks old now, and even though things seemed to be settling into some sort of routine, this time of the night was when it was hardest, when she felt she was just barely keeping her head above the water.

Sometimes she would call Maria or text her older neighbor Sally, who had told her not to hesitate to ask for help. She didn't want to wake or worry Najid, especially now that he had become possessive of his time with their son—their son with a very Persian name, Bahar. Najid seemed completely smitten and was constantly wanting to come over and help with Bahar. She understood it was out of fear and love. He'd lost his precious first family, and now Bahar and she were all he had to hold on to, to hope for as a future. The idea of marriage still scared the heck out of Elizabeth every time Najid brought it up. He suggested that Elizabeth move in; he owned his place, bought before prices skyrocketed in San Francisco. His flat, piled high with pillows and woven rugs and beauty. How would she and Bahar fit in there? Babies were a messy business. And she could be untidy.

When the long periods of breastfeeding and intermittent fussy times took over, Elizabeth imagined herself riding around San Francisco on her Vespa. That all seemed so long ago, before diapers were stacked neatly on her desk, right next to where her thesis used to sit. When would she be able to return to the textiles, to the scents and sounds and history of the Orient? And now, as irony would have it, she was hooked up forever with a Rumi-loving Persian who apparently dealt in rugs, furniture, scarves and cloth from Iran, Pakistan, and what was left of Iraq. She had inadvertently created a family for herself. Her own sister was nowhere to be found. She would love to talk to her, but no phone numbers for her sister worked. And Elizabeth had no idea where she was. Ah, life is not to be understood. She picked up Bahar and offered her breast again.

Elizabeth was amazed that she was all this baby needed, and then terrified that she was all he had—well, except for his father, of course. What happened to impetuous Elizabeth who would throw off her clothes in a second for a good lover, who walked around naked with great pride? Bahar is what happened. Motherhood.

Her body was changing back. Day by day, she could see some of the belly fat disappearing with each suckle from her child. She patted up a big burp from Bahar and looked at him, drunk on breast milk, eyes starting to cross and then close. She laughed as she nudged Bahar back into the blankets of his cradle, right next to her bed. She watched him as his eyelids fluttered and little smiles curled the edges of his lips. It seemed he was having a wonderful dream. Too tired to even turn out the light, Elizabeth heard her own soft breath going in and out as she tumbled back to sleep.

She dreamt of water, warm and soothing, palm trees and a long flat sandy beach covered with coconuts everywhere she looked. She saw a boat in the water, and the last thing she remembered was stepping into the boat, with its wooden sides painted a bright cobalt blue. The boat of herself.

Chapter 26
Surfing Lesson

Sean did leave his coffee cup on the counter, sometimes even the coffee filter, full of grounds, but having always lived in small quarters, he was not much of a clutter bug. Today though, he noticed every dust bunny, every spot on the floor. He was on a clean up mission. MaeAnn was coming over.

He didn't wash dishes except every couple of days, and his frying pan was still sitting out with grease from his last stir-fry experiment, which had actually turned out pretty good. He had added corn at the last minute from a stale cob. He knew the kernels would plump up after they were mixed together with tomatoes and peppers. His foster mother would have called it "succotash".

Last night he was tired after his usual VA appointment, where the docs always put him through a series of brain tests. They banged on his knees with a little hammer and tried to push him to see if he would fall. They ignored that he'd been surfing for years. His balance was still good. While his headaches didn't affect his balance, he usually didn't trust himself in the ocean when he had one.

Finally, he put the last dish away and scrubbed down the counter. He smiled; the place looked tolerable, and he had a few of his better animal photos pinned up here and there, a big cougar over his bed. He hoped it wouldn't scare her out of his bedroom. He'd changed the bed. His sheets were tight; you had to be able to bounce a quarter off them in the military; and it became a habit for him. He was hopeful they would lie on his bed together today, but he didn't want to rush things either.

He had printed out a small picture of the bird's nest with a bit of the pink scarf, Erin's scarf. Erin, he still was trying to find her. He push-pinned the print into the wall near his kitchen. He wanted MaeAnn to see it. He could tell her about the desert and his experience there with the woman, Erin, and he would shorten the story about hiding the scarf so it didn't make him seem kind of creepy. He wasn't sure he quite understood the need to bury the scarf himself, but it had to do with feeling it was contraband, and yet a link to the whole incident, of his being a hero in the story.

He went outside with a cup of coffee in his hand. The surf was faint, with no sign of good waves today. Yesterday, there had been a small earthquake, one that had shaken up everyone in his neighborhood.

Trevor, his geeky neighbor, thought they should check "Tsunami Watch". Later he came by to tell Sean, "No worries, no tsunami, the quake originated in the desert." Sean already knew that, but he let Trevor feel important whenever there was an opportunity because he considered the guy almost clueless. Unless it had to do with computers, Trevor just wasn't connected to life. He thought if he needed more help searching for Erin, Trevor might be his go-to.

Sean saw MaeAnn walking down the boardwalk in a flowered skirt. She looked amazing, but then Sean was totally infatuated with her. He knew that even if she had on the rattiest clothes ever, he would still think that she was beautiful. MaeAnn always had a sense of style, casual, colorful things that popped her brown skin and shiny dark hair. *Oh*, Sean thought, *I'd better stop staring and get out of my chair!*

He and MaeAnn hugged, "Right on time." said Sean.

"Well, I'm eager for this lesson," she said, reaching over to take his hand, "and I'm ready for you too." Then she kissed him lightly on the cheek. Sean felt his knees go a little weak.

"Oh, can I make you a cup of coffee, or tea."

"Oh no, I always have coffee, strong, when I first get up to prepare myself for the day. I'm fine!

"In my family it was my job to make the morning coffee for everybody. I was always the "Lumad" early bird, and I would call out in Tagalog, 'Bunanga ka na handa a na', get up!" She laughed, and Sean just stared at her before he laughed too.

133

"I would love to hear you say that again," he told her, and then she repeated the words. He smiled at her. What a woman, he thought. He wanted to know even more about her family from the Philippines and everything about her.

"Surfing on land?" she asked.

"Yes, I've fixed that all up over here," he said, pointing to the side of his apartment outside. She looked at him and shrugged her shoulders. "Trust me," Sean said, "this is gonna work."

To help her remember her foot placement, Sean had pasted a big pink "X" on his extra board for her at the mid line of the board. "Keep the front foot there until you're ready to do some tricks or want to change directions. It's more stable that way. Your back foot is like your brake; it stays in place." She looked so serious he had to chuckle, which made her look up.

"Is it funny?" she asked. "And the pink, did you use that color on purpose?"

"No, no, I'm sorry, I'm just enjoying myself. I've never taught anyone to surf before. And I happened to have several colors of tape; I just imagined that one would be easy to see." He didn't want to say that he had thought to himself, "Pink, pink is for girls, blue is for boys." Pink was a favorite color of his; he didn't know why, but he saw it as a dominant color in beach sunsets.

She smiled quizzically at him and then lay down on the board, raised up on her arms, brought up her knees and crouched low, and stepped forward, hitting right on the pink X.

"Awesome," Sean said. He couldn't be prouder. "Now, do it again," he said.

In the next hour, her crouch became faster, and her stand better and better. She was really ready for the water now. Of course, today would be the day when the surf was nearly non-existent. And there was a chop, despite the fact that the breeze was only mild, with no real wind to speak of.

They took the boards down to the shoreline and went in anyway. With the water churning, but not really forming any decent waves, he wasn't sure how to teach MaeAnn anything

134

except proper paddling. Still, it felt good to be buoyed up and not doing everything on cement. He saw that MaeAnn could paddle well, her strong arms digging through the water. The two of them paddled out beyond where the normal break line would be. They saw a couple of curious seals bobbing around, and then the seals dove down and came up further out where there seemed to be a small kelp bed. Both MaeAnn and Sean laughed together. There was always something amusing about seals as far as Sean was concerned. He'd seen trained seals in Hawaii when he was on leave once. They balanced balls on their noses and tossed balls back and forth to each other. Sometimes seals and porpoises would ride the waves with surfers.

Sean and MaeAnn kept paddling and turned parallel to the shore and paddled more. Then Sean held onto the tip of MaeAnn's board. He slowly turned her board to face the shore, moving his at the same time. He edged his board over hers and then said, "Okay, crouch up and place your feet. Go ahead."

She looked over at him and smiled. He could tell she was a little nervous too. But then, she did it; she was standing on the water on her board and going with the chop and not falling off.

"Perfect!" he shouted. Then she got back down prone on the board, and they paddled a bit more and finally they came in, riding a little bit of surge that had picked up but not trying to stand. They brought their boards through the foam and then tossed them onto the sand near their towels. They toweled off, and Sean couldn't help taking his towel to dry off MaeAnn's shoulders. She turned and did the same for him.

It was a delicious moment that gave Sean hope for the rest of their day together. He hoped she'd just stay around and be with him all day. He realized when he felt this happy that most of the time, there was often a cloud of loneliness that hung over him. Even though he described himself to others as a "loner," he was happy to not be one today.

Chapter 27
The Message

Najid was getting ready to take the baby on a long walk and was still adjusting the straps to find the most comfortable arrangement for himself and Bahar. Finally, when he turned toward Elizabeth, the front pack snugging their baby facing toward him, he asked her, "Well, what do you think?" Elizabeth couldn't help herself; she laughed.

"Najid, with that round bump of our baby's bottom, you almost look pregnant," she said. Najid smiled at her. She kept laughing, partly out of relief. This was all working out. He did love their little Bahar.

Elizabeth knew she would worry the whole time Bahar was out of her sight, but she found that with all of her time consumed right now with being a mother, she really needed a break. "I'm sorry I won't be walking with you today. I really need some time for myself."

"I understand. You just stay and the two of us shall see the neighborhood sights. It's a sunny day for a change!"

"I think he might just go to sleep when you start walking. Give him the pacifier if he fusses. He just nursed for a long time, so I don't think you'll have to worry about him getting hungry." Najid nodded and turned to go out the door into the sunshine. He looked back and waved. She smiled and waved back.

She went to the table and clicked on her laptop, and scanned two days worth of missed mail. She deleted all ads immediately and then read from the top of the list. Notes from friends who were just hearing about her baby; some were "surprised", while others were "so happy" for her. There were messages from the university with start-up dates for the next semester, and a letter attached from her graduate advisor.

Finally, she came to one from someone she didn't know, "Cleo Green". All that she saw was a string of numbers which

136

made no sense to her. She was about to push the "junk" button when she noted an attachment. She debated with herself; opening these attachments could be dangerous; they could be virus-laden, or phishing. But she had a Mac, and since viruses weren't often a problem, she clicked. Up popped a photo from long ago: an image of her grandmother at her wedding. Grandmother stood in a floor length satin gown with a long veil. In her gloved hand, a bouquet of white roses and lilies. This was the same picture Elizabeth kept on her bookshelf, between volumes of Rumi and other poets that Najid had given her.

This "Cleo" had to be Deirdre! Only she would use the encrypted email device, one which she had spent an hour showing to Elizabeth a few years ago. "We will use this to communicate if there is ever danger," Deirdre had said. Elizabeth couldn't imagaine what that might be, but she had just agreed, and tried to pay attention to the instructions her sister had given her.

Elizabeth pulled out a manila envelope. *All Things Deirdre* written across it in bold, black ink. Tucked inside, on a piece of lined paper in her sister's scrawling script, she found the name of the encryption program, and a note on how to decrypt a message. Deirdre had written it all down for her. Taking the note in one hand, and a pen and paper in the other, Elizabeth followed the step-by-step instructions until finally she pushed, *Enter*, and there it was, the long string of numbers turned into a few terse sentences:

Being followed. Hiding in safe place; you know where. Will call soon. Have to be very careful right now. xo DE.

She knew where? What did her sister mean by that? They had their hideouts as kids, but surely she wouldn't be in San Francisco? Maybe that place on the Russian River they stayed as kids? The house had once been in her grandparents' family. Right on the waterfront, it was now a hotel. Elizabeth didn't even remember the name of the place; all she remembered was that it was painted yellow and had big decks that led out to the river, with ducks swimming along with the current, and fish coming up to grab mosquitoes at dusk.

That must be it. There was a gazebo down the path by the river where she and Deirdre would go to read, and talk about what they were reading. Deirdre would be reading Ursula Le Guin, while she read things like Roald Dahl's *BFG*, or *Are You There God? It's Me, Margaret*, by Judy Blume. She loved Judy Blume books, but her sister read only science fiction.

Elizabeth would have to do a search of all the hotels in the Russian River area and look at the images. Suddenly she felt panicked for her sister. She knew her sister's work led her to jungles and deserts and into areas of biology and botany that not many people entered. But what could be so dangerous that she would be in hiding, and being watched? And now, with her own life being completely focused on a three-month-old baby, fitting Najid into her life, and doing her graphics business too, how could Elizabeth possibly track down, much less help her sister?

She turned and went over to the bookcase and got down the picture of Grandmother Cummings. She took it with her as she sat on her loveseat. "Grandmother, " she said, "help me figure this one out?" She plumped a pillow behind her and while she settled down with a book she'd put off, her eyes closed and she nodded off.

******

In her dream Elizabeth was wearing a white dress and veil, and she was carrying the rose and lily bouquet. Najid stood waiting for her at the alter with two little kids, a dark girl about four years old and Bahar, a two-year-old toddler, who was twisting around uncomfortably to better see his mother walking down the aisle. When she came a little closer, he broke free from his father and raced to grab Elizabeth by the skirts, begging to be picked up. But she couldn't pick him up without dropping her bouquet so they hobbled down the aisle together until Najid reached down and swooped him up, Bahar fussing.

When his father set him back down, the dark child took Bahar's hand and shushed him. She recognized the child now; it

138

was the girl she had seen laughing in several pictures at Najid's place. His daughter, who would always be four. The little girl wore Elizabeth's pink paisley scarf; the scarf swirled around Sonja until she was practically mummified by it; the pink was all Elizabeth saw now as she hurried to take her vows.

Elizabeth woke up in a sweaty panic. Where was her baby? Oh, that's right, on a walk, safely in the neighborhood.

Elizabeth put her book down and stretched. When she got up she noticed that her period had started. What a mess this business of being a woman was, messy and painful and unrelenting all the way around.

Elizabeth stepped into the shower, a little on the cold side since the washer was running. She happily watched as foamy suds went down the drain. While she was washing her hair, she heard the front door close,

"We are back, my sweet." There was finally a knock on the bathroom door. "Are you okay?"

"Yes, yes, okay, just woman troubles."

"Well, Bahar is awake. He got excited seeing all the dogs of the neighborhood, and the kites sailing above the trees in the park."

"Good, that's good. Thank you for taking him, Najid."

"And you have a blinky light on your phone too."

Oh, couldn't she just be left alone to take her shower without the intrusion of the outside world, without the necessity of thinking about a baby and a man and on and on. She cried quietly in the shower and finally stepped out and grabbed a towel.

She realized her hormones were making her moody, and she simply toweled off and pulled on a pair of sweat pants and a long-sleeved T-shirt.

She went out to sit with Najid and to watch as her son flipped himself over and pushed himself up on both arms, rocking back and forth. "He's going to crawl early, Najid. The Dr. told me he's ahead on all his milestones." Najid nodded his head, as if to say, *Of course. He's my boy.* Najid was quietly laughing as he bent over Bahar's kicking legs. Her lover seemed very happy today with his little boy, with being a father again. He put Bahar down on the floor for his "tummy time." Najid picked up the picture of her grandmother in her wedding dress from the loveseat and looked at it, then looked over at Elizabeth.

"You look like her, you know, you really do. And she was a beautiful bride," He gave Elizabeth an intense look, and for a moment, she was both terrified and excited that he was about to ask her again. Marriage. When he turned away without saying anything more, she didn't know whether to feel relieved or disappointed.

Elizabeth was making a simple supper for Najid and herself and she had finished feeding Bahar. Elizabeth was finished with this day, even if her sister could be in trouble. Tomorrow she would be fresh, and she would look into the encryption needed first thing in the morning. Later that evening, as Bahar slept and Najid read from some of his Persian magazines, Elizabeth was on a search for her pink scarf. She didn't know why she was so stressed out by not being able to find her favorite one. Maybe it was that dream of the wedding, the girl with her scarf wrapped around her.

"Aren't you going to check your phone for the blinky light?" Najid reminded her

A lot had happened, a sudden baby, a man who was in love with a baby but still grieving for his first child, and now a crazy message from her sister, which she had not yet revealed to Najid. Maybe it was the thought of Deirdre, the memory of how Elizabeth had discovered that ViJay had gifted both her and her sister with almost identical pink paisley-filled scarves. It was a painful memory, but she understood that her sister was a seductress, and her boyfriend happy to be seduced. Anyway, she reminded herself, she had broken up with ViJay by then.

"Oh, I forgot all about that." Jeez. How could she forget to check messages when her sister had specifically said she would call? Yes, she saw from her phone, she had missed her sister's call, sleeping when she should have been worrying about Deirdre.

140

Then in her messages, there it was, another string of numbers from *Cleo Green*. She would have to do this tomorrow.

She leaned her head against Najid and didn't wake up until he finally nudged her. "Just stay here, she said, "I'd like that. Stay here with me and Bahar."

"What! In your bed?"

"Yes, in my bed. And by the way, I have cramps. It's my time, are you okay with that?"

"I understand about women and their cramps, my love."

"Just cuddles tonight," she looked at him."

"Okay," he said, with the biggest grin she'd seen on his face since the birth of their son.

Chapter 28
A Black Wig

Deirdre sat in her room waiting. It had been way too long. She wasn't really sure what had caused them to drift apart and to spend less and less time with each other, but her sister and she were now leading such different lives. Deirdre's was always on the go, searching for plants—usually the kind others were willing to pay good money for. And when she was home, she had a husband and a growing son to worry about. And then there was her sister, Elizabeth, with her boundless physical energy but rather messy life. They had become very different people.

Deirdre thought about her husband, Mateo. She had met him on a botanical exploration trip in Paraguay. She'd fallen for his charms, good looks, and his own knowledge of local plants and customs. He'd been invaluable on that trip, and then later on, in a different spot, they just started to stare at each other across a bonfire until they finally made mad love in a tent and cared nothing if the others on that trip heard them. She smiled, remembering that day when they hadn't even waited until dark. And now their son, Arguello was a 12 year-old who was growing taller and lankier every day, handsome like his father.

In Long Beach her husband Mateo sometimes went by his first name, John, but unless she was mad at him she never called him anything but Teo. She didn't see much of her husband or her son lately, traveling as she was, and then Arguello went to Montevideo to visit his Uruguayan grandparents almost every year.

Even though his father was pretty dark, with straight black hair, her son's hair was wavy with a red, Viking cast to it, same as her sister, Elizabeth, with her curly red hair. And now Elizabeth had a little boy of her own. Deirdre had a hard time imagining Elizabeth as a mother, with her scattered ways. Changing diapers and tending to a crying infant, spit up and leaky milky breasts, she just couldn't picture her sister dealing with the challenges of motherhood, but she knew she would love her baby. She was fiercely loyal. *Elizabeth would be a mother bear*, Deirdre thought, *protective and tough.*

Today, Deirdre would get to meet this little nephew and hold him close and soak up his baby smells. She felt excited and restless and could feel the uneven ticking of her heart, probably residual damage from what happened to her out in that desert. She shuddered and pushed the memories aside.

She had been in some dangerous situations out in jungles while searching for plants that could be turned into medicines, or ones simply not found in the United States. She loved her work. Nothing made her happier than spotting a new species poking through overgrowth. Deirdre loved the feel of soil as she removed the plant carefully and stashed it in her tote bag, making a notation, where it was found and some landmarks so she could return to the spot later on.

Her sister had always loved books more, and one of their biggest fights had been when Deirdre used *Little Women* as a place to press her plants, collected anywhere and everywhere, into the pages with Jo, Meg, Amy and Beth. Oh how Elizabeth had raged at her until finally their mother, who usually just ignored their fights, made Deirdre buy a new book for her sister, and it had cost a lot of money. Deirdre saw books as interesting occasionally—except for her field guides. Those she had with her in her pockets. Plants and animals took that revered spot in her soul. Well, she did still believe in souls, even though with every experience, especially the one she had endured in the desert, she had come to doubt that everyone had a soul.

Being here on the Russian River had unleashed other memories, happy ones. She and Elizabeth had spent most of their time near or on the water, in a funky old rowboat with chipped oars, sometimes fighting over who would get to choose the direction for a ride, or each taking an oar. Elizabeth was always better, and even though she was younger she had a lot more strength. They had gotten caught a few times on branches or launched too far up a sandbank. They both srained to push the boat back, or sometimes they had to simply wait for the tide to rise a bit to release them. Deirdre chuckled to herself at these memories, some of them so visual: two sun-browned girls, hair flying behind them as they ran to see who would be first into the gazebo, for the best spot to read, without the glare of the sun. Their grandmother took them to the library every week. and set aside a time for reading every day.

Often after a slog through the reeds at the side of the river, the girls would emerge gasping and mud-splattered. The quarters they saved from doing chores for Grandmother were spent at Bartlett's Five and Dime, a short walk away. Nothing was ever a dime, though. They were lucky with their grandmother who went all out for them every summer they stayed with her. She never seemed to tire of their company, even though she was a stickler for manners and helping out. Deirdre had learned to set a table the right way, with the fork on the left on top of the napkin, knife and spoon on the right. She also always said grace before a meal.

"You girls need to recognize what you have, what we all have, and give thanks and gratitude." Grandmother did not require an *Amen,* or a mention of Jesus when it was their turn to say grace, but thanks was required.

Ah, those simple times. Deirdre thought. Exploring the river and finding frogs and plants that she had never before seen, had turned Deirdre toward biology. *Damn, she was good at it too,* she thought. Even all the way through college, including her graduate studies. She knew she was good. She was!

She had seen the sign, "Monte Rio Awaits Your Return," as she had driven in last week. The town much the same; Bartlett's was still there, but the Pink Elephant Bar where they were strictly forbidden to get close to, was condemned, a big sign across it said so. Apparently it was sliding into the river. Slowly. This town was always slow.

144

There were dangers, the river flooding, lately wildfires, and even homeless encampments and shootings. What a mess. But at least here she could think about what to do next.

Deirdre got up and paced; she needed to stretch her legs and to burn off her nervous twitches. Her legs were so restless sometimes she could make holes in the sheets she'd been sleeping on. Her room at the Inn faced out to the street, rather than the river. She needed to watch. She might have been followed here. She missed her husband and son, but they understood that this was necessary for now and they simply texted her and didn't even Face Time. She had been in dangerous situations before, but nothing quite like this with her own people after her. Hector, her former plant partner had sold her out to the big Agribusiness guys—and, in turn, Big Pharma.

She took off the black wig she'd been wearing and looked in the mirror, giving her short short blond hair a quick brushing to relieve the scratchiness. Then she popped the wig back on again.

She saw a rental car pull into the parking lot and recognized the wild reddish corkscrews of her sister Elizabeth right away. And now, with a baby, her own little son, and a man, she'd said, Persian. She really had to think this was entirely like her sister. Predictably unpredictable.

Elizabeth knew to come upstairs and that she would meet her at the top. No one here had seen Deirdre without her black wig. She did a quick adjustment to straighten her hair and took a deep breath.

She wanted it to go smoothly and for her sister's baby-daddy to see her own strength, and to feel comfortable with Deirdre holding his son. She didn't even know the baby's name but she knew it would probably be love at first sight. She looked in the mirror and straightened the wig again, took another deep breath, opened the door and walked out onto the floral carpet to await the little family. Her heart was racing and skipping so she pinched her nose and blew. She waited until she felt her heart even out and then let go of her nose. Vagal nerve response correction: one of many tricks she'd learned from friends who'd been given bad drugs before. It reset the heart.

Now, she was ready. But, she wondered, how could they be ready for her, and her story? Even she wasn't clear on the story—or who it was she was hiding from.

Chapter 29
Monte Rio Reunion

Elizabeth wrapped a blanket around Bahar; the fog was still lifting off the Russian River, the air damp and cool. Najid reached over, took him, and said, "I'll carry the little guy in to meet his aunt."

"Okay," Elizabeth answered as she got out the diaper bag, feeling clumsy as she banged it against the car. She picked up a few little toys for Bahar. She remembered her tote with her phone at the last minute and then slammed the car door shut. She was trembling a little. She was nervous about this whole thing, the introduction of Bahar, not to mention Najid, and then what to say to Deirdre. With only a few friends, no mother or grandmother to confide in, Elizabeth hadn't really talked much about what being a mother was like for her. She didn't even talk to Najid about it, but then he had experienced a lot of it with her. He was very caught up with Bahar, and with being a good father to their son. She felt a certain sense of pride that Najid wanted to carry the baby. She saw it as declaring his connection to the baby and to her as well. Now Deirdre and she had that bond, the motherhood connection.

She had listened to Deirdre's second message, left as a voice message, but it turned out to be just numbers she recited and that name, once again, Cleo Green. Now as she went up to the office clerk at the Inn, she said it as though she had been saying it all her life,

"We're visitors of Cleo Green. Actually, I'm her sister."

The desk clerk smiled, "Oh yes, Cleo, the one with the dark hair and the long coats. I thought she might be a spy," he said, laughing. Her sister could be convincing and charming, but sometimes she overdid it. "Yes, I'll call her room," he said, turning to retrieve his cell phone from a pocket. "Ms. Green, you have visitors, relatives. Shall I send them up to your room?"

Dark hair, long coats—no, that did not sound like her sister, but she stopped herself from saying anything. She just looked over at Najid and Bahar. Najid gave her a hard look, like, *What's up?*

"Yes, she said to come up, and she will meet you in front of her room #12, right up there," the clerk said, pointing to the stairs behind him.

They climbed the set of steep old stairs and then went down a long hallway. This place was rebuilt but looked like something from a hundred years ago with wainscoting and high ceilings. Painted a creamy white with a darker golden-hued trim, she thought that it was really pretty. There was a slight dank smell, but not enough to make her start sneezing. Finally, Elizabeth stopped. They had reached room #9.

"Najid, I need to hold Bahar. I am so nervous. Holding him will give me something to concentrate on."

"But you will want to hug your sister, no, I think I should still hold him." He gave Bahar a little kiss on the top of his head, and she saw Bahar reach up to touch his father's lips. *His little arm and hand are chubby now,* Elizabeth thought.

"Okay, okay."

"You will be fine, Betta; your sister will make you happy, wait and see." He shifted Bahar over, took one of the bags from Elizabeth and took her hand, and they continued down the hallway toward Deirdre's room.

Before they could even knock, the door to room #12 opened, and there stood a woman she did not recognize at first. It was Deirdre all right, but a thinner, paler version with a dark bob. Elizabeth thought her sister seemed okay but a certain look of distress crossed Deirdre's face. When she saw Elizabeth, Deirdre cried out, "Lizzie, oh, look at you and this," she turned toward Najid and Bahar, "This must be your family." Najid dropped Elizabeth's hand and took Deirdre's hand in his. They shook hands. "Yes," Najid answered, "we are her family."

The sisters hugged, their usual strong bear hug. Something their father had taught them and something they always did, seeing who could out-hug the other.

Surprisingly, when Deirdre held out her arms toward Bahar, he reached out to her. Elizabeth knew that her son wasn't always friendly, but with the right coaxing, he could smile. Elizabeth never let others really hold him. Only her closest friends, like Maria.

Deirdre looked him over.

"You are a real sweetheart," she said, touching Bahar's little curls and giving him a kiss on the cheek. Elizabeth looked over at Najid. He had a tear in his eye, which he was wiping away. She knew he could be sentimental. But suddenly she started to cry and turned to get a hug from Najid. Deirdre waited and then handed the baby back to Najid and opened the door to her room.

"What is it, Sister? What is making you cry right now at this happy moment?"

"Oh, I just miss our grandmother, and now that I see you, Deirdre, I realize I've been missing you too, to share my life and for you to meet my little boy." Najid looked at her, "And to meet Najid too." She added, stumbling with her words. *Damn,* she thought, *why did she always got tongue-tied when strong emotions arose.*

Deirdre just laughed and said, "Let me open the drapes. There is a great view of the river from here and now we can all relax." She pointed to her dark hair, and Elizabeth realized she probably wanted to take off what must be a wig.

"Okay, and we have brought a few snacks."

"Great." Deirdre said, "I have a little fridge with some good cheese, and I'll make some coffee for us; the little guy can crawl around...oh, wait....does he crawl yet?"

"Rolls over, just starting to get the idea he may want up on all fours." Elizabeth laughed as Najid put his son down on a thick carpet, which Bahar immediately started to inspect closely.

After her first cup of coffee, Deirdre said, "I know you must be wondering about the wig and everything, the 'Cleo Green,' all of it. Let me tell you as quickly and simply as possible without saying too much that I can't say."

Elizabeth turned toward Najid. Najid said, "Do you want me to take Bahar and leave the room for privacy?"

"No," said Deirdre, "Please stay. I trust you."

Elizabeth picked up Bahar, who nursed and then fell asleep. Elizabeth settled him onto the hotel bed, covered him and put his favorite soft brown dog, Archie, right by his head. As she went to sit on the couch with Najid, he smiled at her, reached over and took her hand for just a minute before she sat. She saw how Deirdre noticed this. She felt so proud of her little family today. She knew hers was not a completely conventional family, even by today's standards, but then Deirdre didn't have a conventional marriage either. Elizabeth had admired her at the time of her wedding to Mateo fourteen years ago. Her sister had married for love in a Latin country, bursting with scents and blossoms, fecund and sexy. Now both Elizabeth and Deirdre were mothers of sons, one almost a teenager, and little Bahar, only at the beginning of life. She and Deirdre might be more alike than Elizabeth cared to admit.

Elizabeth got comfortable and crossed her legs yoga style. She knew her sister's love for a good story, a captive audience. Deirdre, who sat in the one chair, an old Queen Anne armchair covered in a flowery pattern, took a deep breath and began:

"You know, sister, I've been traveling and finding plants for a long time now, over fifteen years, and recently I decided to return to this little-visited place where I had been with Teo. He was my guide on that trip, and that was when we first became a real couple. When I—well, this might sound bad, Najid—but it was when I threw myself at him on a jungle trip. Later, after we were married, Teo told me he'd been waiting for me to make the first move. But that's not what I want to talk about right now."

She might have well have just said it, Elizabeth thought, *these are two lusty sisters.* Najid just looked at Deirdre, gave her a reticent smile and then patted Elizabeth's hand.

"Anyway, I'll try to make this as short as possible," Deirdre continued.

"Going back was exciting, on my own, with my husband's instructions about how to relocate the spots we had explored together in Paraguay. I checked plants in areas reserved for indigenous people. They allowed a few archaeologists and plant lovers such as myself to come in and study. I knew it was a big privilege. Before setting out on the hike into the area, I met with a shaman. He gave me a blessing and then gave me some tips about the plant I was searching for. One I had seen there on our original visit. Ipomoea alba, moon vine, was what I was after. A special variety not yet used in domestic gardens. A moon vine, unlike other morning glories, which only blooms at dusk when it releases a powerful fragrance. More importantly, and more related to my personal story, the plant can give one a hallucinogenic high, a trip. I'd been told that there was one special variety, striated and of a different color than most, and that is what I was trying to locate. It also has less toxins which made it more useful for medicinal purposes too."

Elizabeth gave her sister a look, intense and questioning. "I know, I know. With my history, I should stay away from these temptations, Elizabeth, but I just decided it would be safe and I would be okay and it was a kind of research." Deirdre looked over at her sister as Elizabeth shifted her weight slightly so that her shoulder rested against Najid.

"So I did it. I scraped seeds from the pod as instructed by the shaman who'd given them to me. He'd advised me to make a tea from the black seeds rather than chew and swallow them. The tea I had been given before was made for me by the shaman, and was a pale brown. But this time, I wanted to try it for myself. I got out my simple equipment and boiled the seeds down until there

151

was a dark liquid, much darker than before, and then, I drank a cupful."

Najid looked at Elizabeth quizzically, but Elizabeth just nodded at him and turned back toward her sister.

"In a very short time, what appeared before me was incredible. Ipomoea alba seeds give a fairly mellow high, but I did forget who I was and where I was and what I was doing. Just colors, swirls, and the occasional puma images. Any familiar sense of myself seemed to be gone. I was free of my ego." Deirdre looked down.

"After I came back to reality, I collected a pouch full of seeds to study them more intensely, and I, well, smuggled them back into California. I knew I was taking a big chance, but I had various forms of ID with me, some that identified me as a scientist working with the government, and one even mentioned the Air Force. They were forged, but they had always worked for me in the past. I won't say where I hid the seeds, but it was a clever place." At this, she lightly laughed and then stopped for another sip from her second cup of coffee.

Elizabeth glanced at Najid and raised her eyebrows, just enough for him to see, but trying not to distract her sister. He gave back a slight shrug of his shoulders. Elizabeth knew that Deirdre had the occasional contract with the government for plant research, but that she carried forged military identification with her was a surprise. She wondered what Najid was thinking right now.

"I knew that branches of the government, sometimes even the CIA, had long been interested in chemically-manufactured hallucinogens, but probably didn't know anything about this one from seeds that could, under the right conditions, be grown right in California. Now marijuana is legal, so maybe the other drugs will have their day. Often, though, the military is way out of touch with plants that are considered sacred. They prefer to manufacture their own in a chemistry lab. Remember the 50s, when the CIA used servicemen as guinea pigs without their knowledge. LSD. Remember Mom and Dad and that article?"

Elizabeth nodded. She remembered that their parents had read a story to them from the San Francisco Chronicle. The article was from recently released information about the CIA, and their parents had used this to try to scare the two of them from ever trying LSD. Somehow they suspected that Deirdre and Elizabeth had been sold some blotter paper at a rave; she thought that they must have overheard the two sisters talking about it together the next day.

Their parents had stressed how some of these unsuspecting soldiers had jumped to their death from windows or walked into the sea while hallucinating. Her mother had left the paper on Deirdre's bed to read. Elizabeth just remembered how the music had become magic as everything around her turned into cool colorful patterns. Their parents wanted them to know that if they tried LSD or anything like it, they were bound to lose their minds forever. Good thing they had never found out about the ecstasy they'd taken later on. Of course, by now, being a mother, she could understand the concern. Everyone had different reactions. And little Bahar, well, Elizabeth couldn't even imagine him as a teenager.

Deirdre knew that the military was what she blamed for everything. Or Agribusiness and its greedy grasp for traditional plants. She agreed. Plain bad. Deirdre just looked at Elizabeth for a minute and then crossed her legs and continued.

"I decided to get in touch with my contact in the desert, Hector, someone I had gone to college with and to whom I'd sold a few things before. That was the beginning of a big misadventure which I won't discuss now. Just know that I got to be a liability to this man, and I think that he and some others tried to get rid of me after I refused to tell them where to locate the plants. They had even used a form of truth serum on me. They are probably looking for me now, and I'm just waiting it out a little longer before I go public with the story."

"The meaning of this plant to the locals is secret, and it's old and strong and the plant itself has a fragrance that attracts moths and a few small bats. Those help pollinate their crops, and now, with Los Santos trying to patent every seed ever known, they are a ready customer for anything new like this."

Deirdre bent her head down and silently began to cry, wiping tears off her face with her sleeve. Najid squeezed Elizabeth's hand. She could see by the anxious look on his face, that this might be outside his comfort zone. Bahar seemed to have settled into his nap, lulled by the persistent voice of his story-telling aunt. Elizabeth was slightly worried too; here they were with her own sister, someone hiding out, on the run—and they were here with her, with their baby. Not good.

Elizabeth got up and went over to the chair where her sister sat. She put her arms around her neck and said, "I'm here now, and we will do what you need us to before we have to return to the city. I'm so glad you're okay and that you told us about all of this. It is more than what we were expecting, but we knew something was wrong. I so wanted you to see Bahar and meet Najid. And, of course, I am worried about you and..."

At this, Najid got up and went over to Deirdre. He held his hand out to her.

"I know some of this feeling myself, Elizabeth, the knowledge that you are being hunted, but that is another story. I too will be doing what I can for you." He turned to look at Elizabeth, "Your sister, your 'Lizzie', has made me happier than I could ever have imagined."

"Let's call room service for a little more food," Elizabeth suddenly said. Still breastfeeding, she was often ravenous. A good story, no matter how frightening, always whet her appetite. She picked up the room phone and looked at the choices. Najid was still with Deirdre, his hand on her shoulder, patting it. Elizabeth pushed down any feeling of jealousy she might have as she dialed the number for "kitchen." Then Deirdre and Elizabeth heard Bahar starting to wake up. They looked at each other and smiled.

Chapter 30
On the Run

Deirdre gently brushed her black wig and put it back on. Her head hurt, and her hands were shaking so badly she could barely push her short-cropped blond hair under the long thick bob that was her go-to everyday hairstyle now.

She was still pondering the visit with her sister, her sister's boyfriend Najid, and their little boy. *Bahar*, she thought, *is a darling, but what lies in his future with a father from Iran and his mother a disorganized woman interested in the esoteric?* Deirdre imagined that Elizabeth had no time for the esoteric now, between changing diapers and managing a new love affair and trying to earn some money. Both she and her sister were lucky, though, because their frugal grandmother had left each of them a little money. Not much, but a cushion they could count on. Deirdre didn't need it right now, but she might soon, as her Edible Plant Tours and her foraging for new plants all around the world would have to be put aside for awhile. She had to recover from that time in the desert, from injury and from betrayal.

She hung the "Do not disturb" sign on the outside of the doorknob, put her throw-away flip phone into her jeans pocket and stepped out into the late afternoon sunshine. She bought the phone to be able to communicate with her husband. Maybe she would call Mateo and Arguello later on after a short walk outside. She needed time to think and to clear her head. Right now, she felt like a salmon swimming upstream, up the Russian River. As she turned to pick up her sweater and tie it around her waist, she looked out the window that faced the water. A flash of white, an egret. A big one, the bird's wings slowly flapped up and down as it dipped and then ascended, a small fish wriggling in its beak. *Victory for the bird, but not for the fish. Part of a never-ending bracelet, victories knotted with defeats,* Deirdre thought.

She considered getting a beer, or better yet, a glass of red wine which calmed her trembling hands. Really, all she needed to do was go over to the deck here and sit and sip outside in the sunshine and drink her wine, but the bar wouldn't be open for another hour. Maybe that was good because it gave her time to walk and see what was growing near the river now. She tucked in a small notebook, squeezed it in really, next to meds to help control the shakes, which came without warning. She turned and locked the door, walked down the somewhat rickety stairs and onto River Boulevard.

She decided that she would walk east and go as far as she could, turning onto Bohemian Avenue until it ended at the Bohemian Grove, if she would make it that far. The Bohemian Grove: a place where a smattering of talented and gifted men camped out with the rich and the powerful. They gathered to network, pee on the trees, put on plays, and to "Cremate Care." She'd heard all about it for years from the people who were her grandmother's neighbors next to the Village Inn. One thing she didn't like was the logging that she'd heard went on there, sometimes of first-growth redwood trees. Ecosystems were being disturbed all the time. The Grove and the Village Inn were from the same era, at the turn of the century in the early 1900s. Logging then and logging now; she had seen it many times in the Amazon— what it did to the rest of the forest. No places for salamanders or small fungi to grow and thrive.

She started to feel better the minute she began walking along in the redwoods. The pungent fresh smell of forest, and the sight of the river sparkling through the trees made her feel alive and hopeful again. She took out her phone and found she had one bar of reception and clicked on Teo's number. As the phone rang, she suddenly changed her mind and clicked the phone off. She just wanted to be walking out in nature undisturbed.

She noticed the once blue forget-me-nots everywhere along the roadside had mostly turned to burrs now. They grew among bright white oxalis with just a smattering of pink ones. The usual ferns were everywhere, mostly Western Sword Fern, which loved the damp conditions without much sun. Too bad it was just past the fiddlehead season, the fresh growth of the fern, which she liked to steam and then fry with garlic. Surprisingly Arguello had loved them even when he was little, and he ate the fern tubers she dug up too. Well, what would you expect considering the parents he came from!

The berries would be plentiful by the looks of the blackberry vines further into the woods, blossoms over and the hard little beginnings of blackberries. One thing she had loved as a young girl was picking berries with Elizabeth. They ate quite a few until their fingers were stained purple when they came back home to Grandma's. Grandma made pies and jams with the berries they brought back. That scene played out again and again while they visited in the summer. The memory made her smile, and oddly, made her feel hungry for the first time all day. Deirdre had been so nervous about seeing Elizabeth that she pretty much ate nothing. She just picked at a few things to make it look like she was eating.

As she walked along, she started feeling scared again, it was quiet here with no one in sight, and she wasn't sure just what they knew about her. The ones who wanted her special plant information. She could still be found and taken away; this time, maybe they would be successful at getting rid of her. She turned around and started to run along the edge of the road, picking up speed as she went, trying to avoid uneven parts. The chiming of her cell phone startled her and she jerked it out of her pocket, still running. She saw it was Mateo and as she came to the fork in the road where she could view the yellow siding of the Village Inn she slowed to a walk and answered the call.

"Honey, I think I missed a call from you," he said. His questions always came out as statements. "Everything there is working well?"

"Yes, yes," she panted into the phone, "*Everything is fine, my love.*"

"But you sound out of breath. Are you sure?" her husband asked.

"Si, yes, si, I'm outside. I took a jog, it's all good. Can I call you back in a few minutes? I'm near my place now and need to go to my room."

"Okay, yes, call me back, but in fifteen minutes, I'm going to pick up Arguello at his soccer game."

"I'll call you before fifteen minutes," she said. "Kisses, kisses."

"*Abrazos y besos*," he answered. They always ended their conversations like this, kisses, hugs, kisses, except for when they were having a fight on the phone—but that didn't happen much anymore. She smiled at the memory of the early years of their relationship. Fourteen years ago, things had been so volatile between them, but she smiled remembering the passion in the bedroom.

She put the phone back into her pocket and began the climb up to her room, checking her wig to make sure it was still on straight. She was out of breath and knew she needed to rest, even before going to get a drink to steady her quivering hands and legs. She got out her key, unlocked the door, and turned the knob. Sun was streaming in, but soon there would be a sunset to enjoy. She looked carefully around the room, slowly sliding the closet door open, peering in and then closing it. Nothing. Then she slammed open the bathroom door and flung the shower curtains to the side. All seemed okay.

She had to...she had to look under the bed. She delicately lifted the edge of the bedspread and looked below the bed, only the see dust bunnies. No monsters, real or imagined. Finally, she lay down on the bed and did the breathing exercises she'd been taught, counting the breaths in and the breaths out.

Chapter 31
Bohemian Highway

Najid was carefully rounding another curve while his son slept in the back. He glanced over at Elizabeth and saw that she had her head propped against the window of the car and had fallen asleep. The afternoon with her sister had been hard on all of them.

What a day—it was nothing like he'd expected. It was not simply a meet-up of sisters. It had not been about a chance to show himself in a good light, and for his child to meet his aunt. Najid wondered when he would ever be able to show Bahar to his sisters, and to his old aunties, now on semi permanent lock down in Iran?

What had happened to his country? Over the years it switched back and forth from the mystical poets, like Rumi, and the sacred texts, only to be dominated by one religion, one religious leader, with people expelled and driven out, killed, and women back wearing their daily shrouds. Ugh, he would never understand any of it—all he knew was that he loved the colors and smells of home, the spice of the food, the recitation of poetry, and his fellow Zoroasters.

And Deirdre Erin, hiding out, wearing a wig, taking a false name! He knew about these necessities from his own time on the run, but he didn't really want to get involved and couldn't afford to either. In America, people from his country were all trying to live mostly quiet lives, to avoid attention from the government, to keep from being kicked out and sent back—which for him, would mean nothing good. Super-rich Iranians were busy making business deals and putting yet more money away, sending it home in any ways they could find. Many times he'd been asked to take money with him for family members when he went on a buying trip. He'd have to say no to all of these requests. He was busy with his own missions, his own secrets, and well, he didn't want to think any more about their day in that little forested town, Monte Rio.

As his thoughts drifted, he tried to just enjoy the forest rolling by. *The cypress tree is turning green, drunk with the forest.* He understood Rumi—how nature could feel, how trees could be drunk, how they could communicate. He felt it here in this place like no other, except maybe Yosemite. He'd like to go back up into the mountains and take Elizabeth and Bahar, go hiking and take some pictures and dip his feet into ice-cold waters, "snow melt".

Deirdre was a plant collector, and now that mushrooms and other plants that caused visions were becoming more popular, more used and more studied, he thought she had stumbled onto something more than she said, but he didn't really want to know about it. He'd never done it in front of Elizabeth, but he had his little stash of hashish that he sometimes smoked while he listened to the music of Mitra Sumara. She, and others like her, the blessed sound of Iran before the Ayatolah Khomeini. He had no love for that man and was working to bring back his own faith and to help women like his sisters get back to where they were before all this religious bigotry ruled the country, what his wife Zara had desperately wanted before she was killed.

Americans claimed to be religious and have religious freedom, but the government seemed terrified of people using mushrooms for personal things, like trying to see God. He loved that word entheogenic, holding within it "into the god". Now it's what people were calling the very thing Deirdre had hinted at. Why couldn't people just do as they pleased if it seemed to bring them closer to God, or find out something about themselves or just feel good? He'd never understand. As he drove by a stand of straggly pines, he could imagine mushrooms popping up down below. Mushrooms loved damp. They loved pines.

And where was he going with this rather strange young woman Elizabeth? He was beginning to feel something like the love he'd once known in his marriage, but Elizabeth was awkward about going forward. They had fallen into a pattern. It seemed to suit her as far as he could tell. He was tired of it, though, and would like to be around his son more. Still, he had a life now, a chance to start again and give more meaning to what he did every day. And that made him smile as he drove, trying to avoid potholes that seemed to be everywhere on this road. He would ask Elizabeth again, would Betta agree to marry him? He hoped she'd surprise him and say, *yes.*

He tried to reconsider the words he'd learned as a young boy, the advice to try to strive to be good and do good, but then all the stories of battles confused him. His wife Zara studied hard and she taught him more about the meaning of the symbols of Zoroaster, and now he saw it in rugs, saw it in that pink scarf Elizabeth wore the first time he saw her. He saw it in these tall trees and the jagged line of cypress trees here. Elizabeth had told him they were wind breaks that farmers used. In the Middle East they were mostly used to line driveways and make a clear line that divided properties.

Bahar stirred and then he fell back asleep, but Elizabeth stretched and opened her eyes. Najid felt a great pleasure when she turned toward him and reached over to touch his shoulder. "Good job driver, these roads are a challenge. Where are we now?'

"In the trees. Finding our way out of the forest."

She nodded and smiled and then looked back at Bahar. Mothers all the same in that way, he thought. Checking on the baby. He felt a delicious sensation that he later would identify as true happiness.

Chapter 32
CNN Interview

Deirdre had told Elizabeth that she would be on the news tonight and Elizabeth had promised to watch. Najid insisted that Elizabeth come over to his place to watch her sister on the news with him. "Absolutely, come here," he'd said on the phone, "I don't think you should be alone in this, Betta. I want to watch with you. Anyway, you don't even have a TV!"

At almost ten months, Bahar was starting to get heavy. Najid opened the door and then plucked his son out of the pack, held him up in the air, whirling him around until Bahar laughed. Elizabeth loved to see the smiles on both of their faces whenever they were together. Elizabeth took off the pack and settled onto the couch.

Najid seemed calm and positive, but Elizabeth's mind was buzzing with possible scenarios about Deirdre's appearance on the news—and most of them weren't good. She fished out a little cotton blanket from her pack, and her son's teething toy, the bumpy one he liked to gnaw on, *just like her old dog used to do with bones,* she thought. Teething seemed to go on and on, with drool and fussiness and then a shiny white pearl.

Najid gave Bahar a big kiss before setting him down on the blanket which was next to a big stack of rugs. "Don't worry, it's going to go fine for your Deirdre," Najid said as he turned on CNN and sat down next to her on the velvet couch.

Elizabeth took a deep breath because there she was, her sister, sitting with the newscaster in the background as a news ticker ran across the bottom:

Botanist left for dead in incident over plant information.

Najid looked at Elizabeth, took her hand in his, and tightly closed his fingers over hers. The words continued to flash across

162

the screen as the camera panned onto Deirdre's face, more round now then when they'd seen her in Monte Rio months ago, and no wig. Deirdre's blond hair was growing out. She was dressed in a pale, long-sleeved, moss-green shirt and wore khaki pants tucked into brown leather boots. She looked very efficient and pretty at the same time. She was wearing black-rimmed glasses. Elizabeth had never seen her in glasses, but they helped her sister look contained and professional.

What was Deirdre willing to say to the world about all of this? Her sister seemed to have recovered her confidence and was very different from their visit when Deirdre seemed jumpy, was skinny and wore a bobbed black wig. Deirdre had mentioned that she planned to do this...go public and come out of hiding. "It's the best way to stay safe," she'd said. Elizabeth prayed that it would work and that her strategy was the right way to handle this crazy situation. She heard Bahar chatting to himself, just sounds, not words yet. Elizabeth did not take her eyes off the screen.

"Don't worry, Elizabeth, Bahar is chewing the heck out of that knobby toy, and drool is spilling down onto the blanket. Pretty soon, another tooth. If he fusses, I'll pick him up. You should just watch."

"Shush now. Nej, would you turn up the volume a little?" Najid clicked the sound up.

"Look at you, Betta. Your shoulders are scrunched up to your ears."

She smiled and tried to relax; he was right. She was tense. She held a finger up to her lips, and he did the same to her. *Maybe he's nervous too,* Elizabeth thought.

Now the camera was on both the newscaster and Deirdre.

"Erin, we know you travel around the world collecting and studying plants, and you have a popular blog about plants, but how did something so natural and so innocent lead to what happened to you in the California desert?" The commentator, in a tightly fitted gray suit with a blue tie, paused and then went on, "I understand from the local sheriff that you were found by the roadside and

163

taken to a hospital with a very weak pulse. You weren't wearing anything, either. Do you remember any of this?"

Elizabeth saw her sister adjust her glasses and look down briefly at some notes in her hand. She knew Deirdre had an excellent memory, but maybe it had gotten messed up by what had happened to her—or maybe she just needed the prop. If she looked like the serious scientist, people might listen more carefully. Elizabeth could never stop herself from trying to go into her sister's mind.

Deirdre briefly described her career as a botanist. Elizabeth was impressed with her ability to reduce her years of study into succinct sentences. She had a set expression on her face, except when she smiled as she talked about her job, with another big smile as she concluded: "You see, I've always been fascinated by plants and what they can do for us. I love everything about plants; I guess I could say I love them more than I love people." This comment caught Elizabeth off guard, but she believed it. Her sister was not the warm and fuzzy one.

Deirdre continued. "I'm not saying who was responsible. I don't even know myself, but I had just left a consultation next door to Edward's Air Force Base about a plant that a seed company was interested in. They did not tell me how they intended to use it. The plant causes vivid images and feelings. It's an important part of an indigenous culture." She took a deep breath and continued as the commentator just looked on. "They were not a company I usually deal with—my business partner had arranged the meeting. In the end, I did not agree to sell them my information or cooperate with them.

"As I was leaving in my rented car, a jeep with three men and one woman pulled in behind me. I thought nothing of it at first, but when I turned away from near the base, they were still behind me. As we drove further out into the desert, they finally started blinking their lights and pulled me over. All I remember then was that suddenly the woman took out a syringe, and before I had a chance to fend her off, she stuck it in my shoulder, right through my cotton shirt. The next thing I remember is waking up in the ICU of a hospital, unable to move a muscle or respond to the questions I could hear but not answer."

Bahar started to fuss. He toddled over holding onto the couch and held out his arms. Najid let go of her hand and swooped him up. Rocking him back and forth, Najid stood up and walked away from the couch with Bahar in his arms. He was speaking and singing to Bahar softly in Persian. Then Elizabeth looked over to see him give Bahar his son's new favorite soft brown dog, Tommy.

Elizabeth was distracted only for a few seconds, but the next thing she saw was her sister looking straight into the camera, a close-up where you could see that she was frowning and was plainly disturbed. She did not show any signs of fear, though, Elizabeth noticed; she seemed willing to go on. This had been her idea, she reminded herself, to get the attention of media to protect herself.

"I feel responsible to protect the people who have what the company wants. You see, I don't want..." but Elizabeth could see that the commentator was ready to wrap it up. The sound was cut off from her sister's mic, and the camera suddenly pulled back and focused, a close-up, on the commentator as he said, "I'm sure we will be hearing more about your story Dr. Connelly, but for now we have to go to San Francisco, where a full protest is happening at Union Square."

He had successfully cut off what her sister was trying to say. *But at least,* Elizabeth thought, *now people had seen Deirdre and knew that she was possibly a whistleblower, or at least had a real problem. And they'd probably wonder, why, over some plants? The importance of this plant must be immense,* Elizabeth thought, *that people wanted something so badly from her sister.*

All her sister ever planned to do was know how nature could cure the ills of the world, or bring The Creator, as Deirdre had always referred to her idea of God, closer to humans. Elizabeth felt the same way about art, paintings, patterns, material, the history of the Silk Road and what it meant for the development of civilization.

Elizabeth looked into the television background and saw a tall man in black pants and a long-sleeved white shirt. He was behind, nearly off-screen, as Deirdre stood, and shook hands with the commentator. Did her sister need a body guard now? Or was this like the Secret Service? She didn't feel it coming, but Elizabeth burst into sobs, and Bahar looked up from his toy and started to cry too. Najid, Bahar in his arms, came over to Elizabeth.

"Don't worry; she is being protected. I've been praying for her too." Najid held both Bahar and Elizabeth in his arms while Elizabeth cried even harder. "I'm here Betta, and we are safe here in my place with our son, and your sister will be okay. She is used to dangers."

Chapter 33
The Surf, The News

The summer sun woke Sean early. He pulled on shorts and walked down to check on the surf. Sean smiled, thinking of how MaeAnn had looked in her bikini that first lesson last week. He liked women of every size and shape, but right now, all he could think about was MaeAnn, with her round breasts and well-padded bottom. But it was more than that; he liked being around her. She was considerate and funny. Sean hadn't felt this happy with a woman in years.

She was a good student, too, eager to follow his instructions even though their first surfing lesson had mostly been on land, near the cement alley behind his apartment.

Today's surf held up and was solid. Since it was still early, without the usual congestion of surfers, he figured there would be good sets for MaeAnn and she would get to try everything she had practiced with him. He would call her as soon as he got back to his place, after he'd turned on his coffee pot.

"MaeAnn, it's Sean, time to hit the waves!"

"Okay, Sean, I'm just drinking my first cup of coffee, and then I'll be over in about thirty minutes."

"Don't wait too long; the waves are perfect right now. Slow, steady swells and breaking to the left." He really just wanted her with him because, he thought, *the sooner she was here, the happier he'd be.*

"Okay, I'm coming, coffee cup in hand," she said. He clicked off his phone. While he made himself a cup of coffee he practically shook. As he sipped his brew he thought—not only was this a chance to be with MaeAnn, but to watch her really standing and maneuvering through the water. He also wanted to show her his photos, especially of the ravens, their nest. Once again he thought of that pink scarf, that woman who still haunted him.

He was protective when it came to women. He'd seen too much in the war zones—women struggling to keep it all together for their families, not necessarily with good outcomes. Often the men, skinny and tough, could be very rough on women A soft tapping at his open door startled him out of his memories.

"Hey Sean, I wasn't sure you heard me walk up. I didn't want to disturb you. You seemed far away."

"I was, but now I'm here, and I've got your board and mine ready to go. All we have to do is wax them a little once we're ready to go in the water." He stood, took MaeAnn's empty cup and set both their cups on the counter. They walked outside, where he had both of their boards standing against the stucco wall of his apartment.

"Thank you for taking off that big pink X," MaeAnn said, laughing.

He loved to hear her laugh; it reminded him of a cascade of falling water.

She picked up the smaller board, a small echo of an X remaining on the top. *She carried it under her arm like a pro*, Sean thought. He noticed that she seemed confident.

They waded out through the foamy water until they could lie down on their boards and paddle out to the break line, then up and over, pushing the boards before them into the crest of the wave. They popped out the other side and paddled further, and turned. The swells were regular, fairly small, but insistent. MaeAnn looked over at him. He nodded, and they both started to paddle until the surge pulled their boards along, and then she did it; she crouched and put her foot just as he had taught her. This first wave they would just ride in, no leaning into the break but just coasting, and then suddenly Sean flipped off and turned his board back toward the waves, and she did the same. Out they went again, over and over, for two hours.

She was getting steadier with her crouch each time and was starting to use her arms for leverage. She could feel it now, Sean thought. Suddenly he hit a patch of debris which almost tossed him off his board, but he regained his balance, and just then, a seal popped up between them, flippers sending the seal on a good ride too. Last week seals, this week too. Sean thought it a good omen. He brought his hands together for a second. Silent applause for MaeAnn like he'd seen Buddhist monks do when he'd been hiking in Tibet. She just smiled and turned to carry her board through the foamy water to the sand.

They dragged their boards in and up onto the beach. MaeAnn flopped down onto the sand. "That felt so good, but I think my legs are shaking a little, and in my arms, well, I feel muscles I didn't even know I had."

"You'll build new muscle. All that waitressing, your arms are already strong, just in slightly different ways. You were amazing out there MaeAnn. I feel very proud of you today."

"Thank you for helping me." She reached out and took his hand.

They sat up and watched as surfers waded out; Sean saw that the break had picked up a little as an off-shore wind stirred the air. And then there was a fuss out in the water. Nothing to worry about, Sean saw, just a school of porpoises diving through the waves. He looked over to see if MaeAnn had noticed. Yes, she was smiling and rubbing her upper arms. He thought she looked content. That's exactly how he felt.

They carried the boards back to Sean's, and then MaeAnn explained that she had the whole day off. "Are you hungry? I know I sure am," Sean said. " Let's go up the boardwalk to that place where they serve breakfast all day long."

Sean craved a Mexican omelet, huevos rancheros, with green onions, beans and a cheesy sauce, and with plenty of bacon on the side. Maybe even some fruit, since it was melon season and he loved juicy round cantaloupe best of all.

As the waiter brought them coffee, the sports news was on; the women of the USA had just won the soccer finals again, Sean high-fived MaeAnn, and then the regular news started. Sean took a sip of his coffee, hot and strong. Normally Sean was good at tuning out the news. He hated hearing the stupid things the government had done and the usual rants about who the USA would invade next. Unlike a lot of former military guys, he had no desire to pick up a weapon again. Always, he thought, war over a final and rather futile search for oil. Soon it would be wars over water and then maybe even air. But something about the news commentator and the banner caught his attention.

Botanist left for dead over plant information.

MaeAnn was asking him something but he said, "MaeAnn, I have to hear this, I think this might be connected to what I told you before. The desert, the woman." She gave him a quizzical look. Oh, he hadn't even shown her the picture yet, or shared that bit of shredded pink material with her. He didn't remember if he'd even mentioned saving the stranger in the desert. Maybe he had just day-dreamed it all. Reality and dream life often seemed the same to Sean.

Both of them turned their full attention to the news. And suddenly, everyone in the restaurant was quiet as they all listened to the TV commentator.

Sean couldn't believe it. There she was, except her hair was shorter, and she looked, well, different with clothes on, and her serious manner surprised him. She was wearing glasses. Sean could barely breathe. This was that moment of truth, that moment he hadn't expected but had hoped for. Now he might have a way to connect with her, if the news media would give him anything further. But at least for now he saw with his own eyes that she was okay; she had survived and was telling her story.

He believed there was a lot more to it, and that is what the commentator was afraid of. He noticed, it seemed obvious, that she was being cut off before she really had time to tell her tale. He knew there were big guns involved or she could have said more.

She did mention her husband, also involved with plants. Had she meant to say his name, Mateo? And he saw a heavy-set man for a few seconds off to the side of the TV camera.

"Security," Sean said out loud.

MaeAnn looked at him, "Security?"

"Sorry MaeAnn, I have an important story to tell you about this woman, but I can't do it here. Could you come back with me to my apartment? It won't take long."

"Sean, now I really want to understand what is up with you and this woman. She seems to be coming out on TV like a whistle-blower, like she has to protect herself. I know you're not really involved, are you, Sean?"

Sean saw the worried look on her face. He said it as softly as he could, but so she could still hear, "Well, I am involved, but not in a bad way. In a good way. I will tell you everything MaeAnn, so you'll understand. I agree. She is trying to protect herself." He was starting to get a headache. The stress was getting to him.

Now he had to find her. Sean thought. He noticed MaeAnn was staring at him. "Oh, my God, MaeAnn, it is her. I'm going to find her after all." He said this louder than he meant to, and the people at the next table turned to look at him.

"Sean, I'm sure you will. You're a person with determination, more than anyone I've ever met before."

"You see MaeAnn, she didn't mention it," he whispered, "but I am the one who found her left for dead. I was the one who called 911, and the rest, I'll tell you when we get back. "

He took a sip of orange juice and felt that today, at least, he was a lucky man. And after their meal, he would take MaeAnn into his confidence. He thought briefly about how he might also take her into his bed, but he let that idea slide away. He looked over. She stopped eating and gave him a hard look.

She's trying to figure me out, Sean thought as he started on the eggs. While he was hungry, he found it hard to focus on the meal. He hurried through until soon he was paying the bill. "Let's go MaeAnn. That news show really has me rattled and I need to tell you the whole story. I need a confidante to help me sort it all out."

"I can't believe that you are the one who found this poor woman. Now I'm worried about her too," she said quietly to Sean.

Sean opened the door for MaeAnn, and they walked as rapidly as they could back to his place, the sound of big surf crashing around the beach as the tide rose practically up to the top of the boardwalk.

Chapter 34
Boteh Jegheh

Elizabeth was at Najid's place. He had unlocked his safe and was gently taking something out to show her. She recognized it from her studies--a Safavid helmet dating back to 212A.D. The helmet delicately woven iron cloth, a fine chain mail to protect the ears, and a teardrop paisley welded to the top of the metal helmet to proclaim the warrior's belief. *The warrior would have believed in Zoroaster, and in what that little teardrop stood for,* Elizabeth thought. Najid stood smiling and holding it out for Elizabeth to inspect.

"May I take a picture of this for my thesis, Najid?" she asked as she pointed her phone. Najid nodded as she focused in on the armor and clicked a few pictures.

"Just don't mention me as your source," he said. "This will belong to Bahar someday, and I'll explain to him all the history of my Persia, which I hope he will see for himself. Once things settle, once I am allowed more freedom to travel there, I can take him. I would love to take you there too, to meet my old aunties and my sisters. This helmet has been in my family's possession for hundreds of years."

"I love that there is a little paisley on the top of the helmet," Elizabeth said.

"You will see this *Boteh Jegheh* on so many things and in places, not just Iran, but Afghanistan and Turkey and so many other neighboring countries." *Just more proof,* Elizabeth thought, *of how things moved up and down countries, through seaports and on the clothing and jewelry and into the ideology of the peoples of the old Orient.*

"*Boteh Jegheh*?" Elizabeth asked.

"Yes, what you call paisley," Najid answered. She could tell that he was waiting for her to say something more.

"Yes, a paisley, I know how much you like them. I see them on your import-export business cards and on your website. And as for the helmet, it seems precious and ancient, and I'm still trying to imagine that some day it will belong to Bahar." Elizabeth didn't really know how to react. This was quite a precious object, and she wondered if Najid should even have this kind of thing in his possession. Weren't there laws about artifacts? And Najid had a safe. While this fact surprised her, she often felt that she would never solve all the mysteries surrounding this complicated man. He turned and quickly set the combination to the safe's lock.

"I just wanted you to know about this," he said as he turned toward her. *The look in his eyes seems so very serious,* she thought. "Thank you, Najid. We have to trust each other, Nej".

****

Back at her place, Elizabeth was finally working on her thesis again. So much had happened; her life had completely changed, and now her desire to finish her thesis was rekindled. She was cutting and pasting a picture of Najid's Safavid helmet, "one worn by the Persian warriors in 212AD," onto a page of its own. The little teardrop, the seedling, the bent cypress tree showing the sorrow of the Persians after they'd been conquered by the Arabs. The fire, the flame, the everlasting Paisley. Now she could also refer to it as the *Boteh Jegheh.*

Elizabeth sighed as she re-wrote the second sentence of the paragraph. Would she ever finish this? At least now, she had returned to her thesis with a passion which she credited to her love for Najid, and the things he loved. She printed the pages she'd been working on and sat down to edit.

She wondered if she should even mention the current use of the paisley, sewn onto cowboy shirts, on the clothes that flamboyant Oscar Wilde once wore, woven into pashminas like the scarf she had and the one Deirdre had at one time, before the desert must have claimed it. And these days, young people with capes and skirts and tattoos, all with the little bent cypress trees, the little cypress seedling shapes. People and their connections to nature, always, no matter what. And the Zoroastrians, it had all started with them and their beliefs. It stood for life eternal. She had known that even before she had taken up with her lover, Najid, and they'd had a baby, and she'd sold her Vespa.

Elizabeth heard Bahar softly babbling in the other room. She turned off her laptop, got up, stretched and walked into the other room to see what it was he wanted. Nap time over, he wanted up and that would end her own study time. Her thesis writing time, over and done with for now. She'd let him sleep long this afternoon. Now it was almost dark out.

Bahar was banging on the side of the crib with his wooden rattle. He was trying to say words. He was standing up and holding on to things. He was about to walk any day now.

She lifted him from his small crib, and he grabbed at her hair. "Not Mama's hair," she admonished, taking his hand down. But soon she was fake biting and nuzzling her son, and they were both laughing like crazy. Her little Bahar. Najid's little boy. She put him on the bed to change his diaper and snuggle him into a onesie, one Maria had given her, covered with whales on a fishy background. Elizabeth laughed every time she put this onesie on her son, reminded of the day her water broke on Pier 30 with whales breaching in the background.

Elizabeth had printed out some words and put the quote into a frame which hung on her office wall. She and Bahar looked at together every day, the tree on the left with a circle of stars above it, and then the words, a quote from Rumi which she read to him each time they walked by.

Bahar sputtered, trying to get out the word, "star" as Elizabeth pointed to the words and recited them to him. He loved hearing these words and he smiled every time she said the words. He pointed toward the sky and he kick his feet. She knew that meant: *read it again.* And she did:

> *The mind, this globe of awareness, is a starry universe*
> *that when you push off with your foot,*
> *a thousand new roads become clear, as you yourself do*

Then Elizabeth pinched Bahar's bare little toes. He pushed her hand away. And she would do it again, saying, "Foot, toes."

"Da?" he would ask. "Yes, he will be here soon."

She wrapped her pink paisley pashmina around both of them as they walked outside. On a clear night like this one, her son pointed to the moon and pointed to the constellation of Orion, and then they sang a little Farsi song that Najid liked: "*Laay laay laay laay, gole-e-laleh,*" a lullaby often sung to children in Iran, Najid had told her.

It was fall and the sun went down earlier and earlier. She was going to make dinner, as Najid had taught her, a simple saffron rice with vegetables. Even Bahar would eat some of it now. *Najid will be here any minute,* she thought.

She stirred saffron into the rice and turned it down to steam. Just then, Najid knocked, opened the door, and walked into the kitchen. He set down a luscious-looking dessert. When she looked closer at the cake, like a tower, but simple, with candied flowers thrown into the thin icing. She recognized the Persian Love Cake. *Someday, he would teach her how to make it,* she thought.

"Ah, I know what we are eating tonight, my love. It smells delicious. Hey, Bahar," he said, lifting him off Elizabeth's hip."Come here, little guy! How about a ride on Daddy's shoulders."

Elizabeth set the table and looked over. It was clear that Najid and Bahar loved each other just as she loved them. "Loved," she had actually thought the word. She smiled. Things were changing for her every day.

She moved the Persian Love Cake to the middle of her little table. The cake was spicy with just the right amount of sweetness, and the legendary tale, *if you take one bite,* Elizabeth reminded herself, *you will fall in love. It was true!*

Elizabeth went over to hug Najid, who had just put Bahar down where he could stand next to a chair, hanging on with one hand. *Soon he will take off as a full-on walker. Leaving part of babyhood behind,* Elizabeth thought.

Najid said, "I'm so glad I met you, and that the Persian Love Cake worked for us."

He smiled at Elizabeth and she nodded in agreement, "Yes, yes, for sure. We both should have big slices of cake tonight. Even Bahar." Najid laughed and then nodded. "Yes, family cake time."

Chapter 35
The Connection

Sean got out his laptop and banged away until he had what he wanted, a connection that might lead to Erin. It was her husband's email: *Teo@beachgardens.com.*

He sat and thought for a minute. *How do I get into this guy's head? What would be a safe message to send? Guy to guy?*

He began composing a short message. *Most men don't like to read long emails,* Sean thought. In fact that was true for most people now.

Hello Teo:

I am not a candidate for a garden, but I would like to meet you regarding a situation too delicate to put into an...

"Oh no," Sean said out loud, "This is **not** a good start."

He erased everything but the greeting.

Sean was wary of the internet, with all its spying and tracking and everything else; maybe he would just try to come in as a landscaping client...but how would that get him to Erin?

He went outside for a minute to listen to the sound of the waves, big today. The beginning of hurricane season in Mexico and beyond. *Expect 25-foot swells,* he thought. Even though he was not that fond of big-wave surfing, it was fun, exciting, really, to watch other surfers go for it.

He might call MaeAnn and encourage her to paddle out with him into the swells. So far, they were only about 10 feet and that was very doable. MaeAnn was improving every time they surfed together, and each time he was able to give her one or two pointers, just enough so that he did not discourage her. Things like how she could lean into a wave to catch a ride through a tunnel, if the waves were good, and how to use her arms as continual ballast on a bumpy ride.

Leaving the front door open, he sat down again at his old table and began all over.

Hello Teo.

I wonder if I could meet with you to discuss my needs. I live at the beach further down the coast, but I'd like to come to Long Beach to meet with you in your office. I need a full plan. I'd like to see examples of what you've created before.

Yours sincerely,
Sean Quinlin

He got up and wiped sweat from his forehead. He had gotten hot, but then he noticed it was only a 70-degree day outside. His phone told him so. He thought it might be nerves. He was getting closer and closer to meeting the woman from the desert, and that excited and terrified him, that small piece of her pink scarf tucked in a box in his bedroom. How many months had it been now? Maybe even a year?

Before he had any more time to think about it and change the message again, Sean flung the email out into cyberspace. *Even in Afghanistan, people had cell phones, laptops,* Sean remembered.

Instead of calling MaeAnn, he took out his big camera bag and slung it over his shoulder. He reached into his cupboard for the box of *Kind* energy bars and tucked one bar into the pocket of his shorts. He wanted to walk the beach looking for just that right shot, with the sun glinting off the foam or with the seaweed dark, and just a pattern through the wave, like a ghost surfer. *Bull Kelp, disappearing from some of California's coast,* Sean thought

He hoped when he came home there would be an answer to his email from Teo and that he could meet him, and that would lead him to Erin and stop. *Stop!* He had to do this to quiet his spinning brain. A trick he had learned from a therapist or two.

He would get his mind free of Erin, of MaeAnn, of anything but being with himself in nature and seeing if he could

179

capture a moment that showed the awe he experienced almost every day here at the beach. *Abby, would be proud of him,* Sean thought, as he locked his front door and walked slowly toward the ocean. He finally knew how to take care of himself.

He walked past some driftwood and dried kelp washed up in the last storm. Someone had already made a small construction from the sea gifts, and he stopped and focused his camera on the wood grain and then back further, the whole structure, pretty cleverly woven together and with a ragtag door covering, some old fabric that had faded, but still showed a pattern of a big sunburst.

Then he stepped over the carcass of a seagull; they were often on this beach. Once again, the bare white bones with just a few feathers moving up and down, as the sea breezes caught them. He changed the setting again on his camera and then took out his phone to just get some quick, simple shots. Sometimes his phone camera was almost as good as his old Nikon. He walked down to the sand, wet and hardened and in undulated patterns all down the shoreline. *Now these patterns by nature will make a good shot,* Sean thought.

He stepped into the foamy water. He focused the camera lens on the sand patterns with the view from the sea toward the land. He noticed that the water was pretty warm. *El Niño,* he reminded himself, everything about the water was affected. *The amount of moisture in the air, the sea creatures that came in closer, or not, and the sky itself even seemed different,* Sean thought.

Ah, nature—always complicated, but he felt more familiar with it than he did with most humans. MaeAnn was in his life, and she added sparkle. He could just be himself around her, but his best self, of course. He smiled because he was feeling thankful for his life with her in it.

He turned to walk back to his little apartment and make a quick meal and try not to obsess about a possible email reply. The air smelled salty and slightly fishy. Smells he had grown to love.

Chapter 36
Deirdre and Mateo

Deirdre was on the phone with Mateo. He had gotten a message from a potential client.

"I thought you took down your site after my TV appearance, like I did," Deirdre said.

She didn't want to seem angry, but she felt a prickle anyway. He could be casual about things. She realized that they'd had so many separations over time, with her traveling and him taking care of Arguello; he didn't always listen to her now. He no longer reacted intuitively, the way she'd like him to, as he'd done at the beginning.

"I left my banner up and my email contact. I can't just abandon my clients. I have to figure out someone who can take over. And we can use the money when we get to Uruguay. You know mi madre."

Yes, thought Deirdre. She did know how his mother could be—a half-indigenous woman with an Italian husband. A woman who tried to hide her background, but who still had her potions and her rituals. *A woman who cared very much about appearances and status,* Deirdre thought.

She looked out her hotel window near the airport, in the financial area near Newport Beach. John Wayne was a small airport and less watched by people likely looking for her.

"Okay, I understand what you're saying about your work, Teo, and I know it's hard for you to let it go for the time being, but we have talked about this ever since the incident since I was so messed up. We both agreed to leave the country for a time and to go out of reach of the media."

Then she took a breath and thought she still had her blog up, but it said that it was not an active blog. Still, she could not completely remove it. She, just like her husband had worked hard

182

to build up something, and it was not easy to just let that go. Now that Deirdre had appeared on TV, she noticed that searches for her name were sky-high. And she secretly looked at the visits counter on her website, thousands every day. But she must take it down, even though the contact information was already cut off.

"Okay, we have our plans in place, don't we? I have my plane ticket, and you have yours. Did you contact your parents? Did you let Arguello know we are joining him there?"

"Yes to all questions, Deirdre Erin. I am super protective of you."

Mateo texted Deirdre in the middle of the night. *"I wasn't completely honest. I'm meeting with the guy. It seems like he wants to tell me something important about you, and not get a garden plan. On the phone he says he has something to prove that he was that guy in the desert who called for the ambulance."*

"Oh Good God!" Deirdre yelled. Deirdre's heart beat so fast she knew she needed to take a pill to calm her heart and herself. Would this lead to more complications? She turned on her bed lamp and sat up.

"Okay over there?"   "Yes Jimmy, 1010, yes." She'd remembered to dial in the code they'd agreed on. Deirdre just needed to get out of California as quickly as possible. She thought for a minute, and then she texted back: *Okay, after you meet him, if you think he is the real guy, maybe I should meet him too? Maybe he can tell me more details about how I was when he found me.*

Deirdre, don't worry, I will be cautious; we are meeting down by the pier near our home, but outside and where I can scan the distance for anyone else, anyone who seems like a threat.

I am worried, and you know how I am now; anxiety can really trigger all my aches and pains, but I think you'll come up with a good plan. I trust you. I'm glad you told me!

I just didn't want you to fret too much. I know it's the right thing to do. He may be of some help to us in all this. I love you and miss you more than ever. I know you are safe where you are, but soon we must go. I worry too, you know. I do not want you to meet this guy at our place. Let's talk about this later. Love you, Teo.

Deirdre turned off her phone, got up and walked into the next room. She was quiet, as she did not want to wake the security guard posted in the other part of the suite in the hotel in Newport Beach. Jimmy was someone Mateo had known from Uruguay, and he seemed perfectly suited: quiet, attentive, and big. But then she dropped her phone, and it clattered onto the kitchen floor. Jimmy had heard the phone drop and texted her, *Everything okay in there?*

She quickly texted back, *Yes, 1010,* Deirdre punched in the code that they had worked out to make sure he knew it was really her.

"Okay, I'm here," Jimmy texted back.

At first, she didn't think that she needed a guard, but Teo insisted. While she felt safer after the interview, where Jimmy had first been with her, Teo didn't see coming out to the media as a solution and wanted Jimmy to stay with her to make sure she was safe. They still had no idea who, exactly, caused Deirdre to be left by the side of the road unconscious. The dark side of medicine wasn't always kind to people like her who wanted to develop drugs that would help people from new plant sources without taking away the lives and the forests, and everything from the people who lived with the plants and knew their uses.

She felt grateful for her friend who had convinced the TV station to interview her. At least the story was public now, or at least as much of the story as she knew.

She sighed and popped a yellow pill and then a white one. They would help her relax. Just one more day and she would be on a plane out of here.

Deirdre curled into the fetal position with her arms down between her legs. She didn't think. She didn't even dream. She just fell all the way into a deep slumber.

Chapter 37
The Promise

Elizabeth was sitting outside in the yard brushing tangles out of her curls. Bahar was walking around, falling every few minutes. She could see that he was a determined child who always found something to hang onto as he tried to pull himself up. Sometimes it was a plant that surprised him when it gave way, and down he went again. Mostly he laughed. *He is a good-natured little guy,* she thought. *With two intense parents, where did he come from?* Elizabeth laughed at the ironies of life.

Najid was on his way over, and Elizabeth was really looking forward to seeing him, being with him, looking into those eyes of his. Bahar's eyes would be like his, brown with hazel flecks. Elizabeth found herself becoming more sentimental, a quality she never really found appealing in other people. Was this what being in love, what being a mother, did to you? She finally put the comb and mirror in their case and was starting to get up when Bahar looked toward the door and suddenly smiled.

Elizabeth turned to see Najid with outstretched arms, welcoming Bahar to walk, or even try to run, into his arms. When he did, Najid tossed his son up into the air and caught him. When he sat down next to Elizabeth, Bahar tugged on Najid's chin, on the little goatee Najid had started growing. Bahar wriggled to get down again.

"He just can't get enough of walking," Najid said, smiling. "Little Sonja was like that too, always in motion." Then under his breath, Elizabeth heard him say something more.

"Haroomzādeh!"

"What, Najid, what did you say?"

"In English, it means *bastards*. Those who took my family away. It sits heavy on me. I want to have my revenge against them.

Even though I have tried, I still do not know who to blame, so I just call them "*Haroomzādeh*!"

He pounded his fist against his thigh. Bahar looked up. Elizabeth didn't really have a reply, so she took his hand. Then she kissed his cheek.

"I understand how much it must hurt to remember these things, your other family."

Just then, Bahar picked something up and started to put it in his mouth. "A eucalyptus seed pod," Najid said, as he quickly took it away and tossed it over the fence.

"He loves these seed pods, we always talk about how there is an "x" in the pod, but he usually does not try to eat them," Elizabeth said.

After a moment of being very quiet, Najid said, "You know, Betta, I have spent a lot of time looking into who is responsible for this act against my family. Although I don't think they targeted my family, it was more of a political thing. Zara and Sonja happened to be wrong place, wrong time. Many others were killed too. I was doing business only a few blocks away. It was all so quick and violent."

Elizabeth shook her head. "I am so sorry, Najid. I understand how deep this goes for you."

Najid wiped his eyes, and Elizabeth saw him physically shake off these memories.

"You know what,"Elizabeth said, "let's take a walk with Bahar. He seems like he needs to calm down before dinner. And we could take him to the corner place and catch a bite to eat there, look at the stars from that garden."

"Okay," Najid said.

"Let me get sweaters for Bahar and for me." She turned toward Najid as she let go of his hand and said, "Promise me you won't do anything to jeopardize what we have together now."

"Yes, my love, I promise. I will always be aware I have a new family and a much-beloved family too. I would do nothing that would mean I would lose you and Bahar. Never, I promise."

186

Elizabeth picked up a sweater from her bed and as an afterthought, wrapped her favorite pink scarf around her shoulders. She felt pretty tonight, and loved. The scarf made her think of Deirdre.

Elizabeth knew her sister would soon be out of the country. Mateo had messaged Elizabeth. She was more connected now; she had her sister back again. She imagined that despite the age difference, their two boys, these very different cousins with several cultures involved, someday would be buddies.

Najid said, "Let's use the stroller. The fog might roll in, and it would be warmer for him. And also, he might just fall asleep." He gave her a wink.

Elizabeth smiled. She imagined it as almost a date, that's what he meant too. Like dates they used to have before the lively chaos of Bahar came into their lives. Tonight she and Najid would click their wine glasses together and savor the moment, celebrate their luck, their *kavarenah* finding each other. She locked the door, and the little family strolled toward the corner. There was no hint of fog, only the last remnants of sunset lighting the sky a pale rose color. Her scarf fluttered on the breeze, so Elizabeth tied the ends together, and now everything seemed just right.

Chapter 38
Meet Up

Deirdre sat in her hotel room writing notes to herself. She tried to put herself back into that terrible day in the desert. The real puzzler when she obsessed about that day in the desert was why, except for the pink paisley scarf she'd brought for the cool night air, she'd had on no clothes. That's what she had been told.

Was she raped? There were problems with that recently. The military struggled to control the problem. And she had been close to a base. *She might never have the answer*, she thought, as she put her notebook under a pillow on the bed of her room. She needed to repack her bag, her flight would be leaving late tonight, and she wanted to remember everything, and not leave any traces behind.

If that person, whoever he was, had not found her in time, she would be dead now, but here she was alive and in a room next door to a bodyguard, waiting to get on a plane to Mexico and then on to Uruguay. She was trying to stay safe. She was not sure why they'd wanted to kill her, but that scared her. She was afraid, even after going on TV to discuss what had happened to her. She had let out a big groan that Jimmy heard.

Everything okay? Jimmy texted.

Yes, sorry, that was me getting ready for traveling, trying to relax. I'm fine, thank you. She realized she had forgotten to punch in their code, "1010" so he knew it was really her texting. Deirdre just shrugged her shoulders. She couldn't really think straight right now and everything was in a state of flux.

After she hung up she noticed her blinking light, a message from Teo.

"Sean wants to meet you, and I think it is fine. It's okay, go ahead and see Sean; he's safe. I've changed my mind. I think it might be good for you to meet him. I trusted him right away and

you will too. I have given him your hotel room number and the name you are under at the hotel."

She tossed the phone into her jacket pocket. And put her notebook down on the bed, under her pillow.

As she got up, vertigo made her remember the ride at the fair with its slow whirl, one she always hated but was pressured into taking. *She never wanted to show any weakness.* She knew this had gotten her into plenty of scrapes when she was young. Suddenly, her phone rang. She answered and waited for the other person to speak first.

"Hello, this is Sean. Your husband Mateo told me you were here. I have something to show you, very important. I'm the guy who found you in the desert. My name is Sean Quinlin."

"Tell me a little bit more," Deirdre said, her heart pounding.

"Your husband Mateo wanted you to know that now he has taken down his blog, I'm the last person to contact him, and it's okay for you to talk to me. Maybe you'd be more comfortable meeting me downstairs, in the lobby?"

"Yes, I need a minute. I am going to ask someone from the front desk to send up an escort, and then I will meet you downstairs. How will I know you?"

"I surf, I'm very tan and tall, and I'm part Native, so my hair is very dark and straight and a little on the long side. I will be the one who looks very happy to see you alive and well."

Deirdre's hands started to shake uncontrollably. Maybe she had nothing to lose.

"OK, Sean, I will look different than I did on television. I have dark brown hair now. I will be down in about 10 minutes, as soon as I can get an escort." *No more itchy black wig, no more cropped blond hair,* Elizabeth sighed quietly so that Jimmy would not hear her.

"Erin I am happy that you'll see me."

"And Sean, my name here is Cleo, Cleo Green."

Deirdre hung up, and pushed the button on the phone for the concierge.

189

"I want to come down to the lobby, but I'm a little unsteady on my feet; could someone come and help me down the stairs? I'm afraid of elevators."

This was a high-end hotel, with a lot of older guests, a lot of famous guests, Deirdre had noticed Julia Roberts leaving with someone carrying her bags. *They were used to accommodating their guests*, she thought,

"A young man will be right up."

Deirdre clicked on Jimmy's phone number. First she punched in the number, 1010, as she was supposed to.

Everything okay Deirdre?

Jimmy, I'm getting an escort down to the lobby. I'm meeting someone there whose name is Sean, and Mateo says it's okay.

There was a long pause. *Don't you want me to come with you?*

No, you look too much like a bodyguard. I don't want to draw any attention to myself.

Well, I am your bodyguard, Jimmy practically snorted when he said this. She had insulted him.

I'm sorry, I've felt very safe with you nearby, and I want to make sure you're here until it's time for me to get on the plane.

I won't be going anywhere. Take your phone and call me if you need me; also, tap on my door when you return so I know everything is okay.

Yes, I will, Jimmy. Thank you. Don't worry. She said this as much for herself as for him. Deirdre dropped her phone back in her pocket and slipped on her boots. She quickly ran a comb through her hair.

"Okay," she said to herself, "Here we go." Just then, a knock on the door, and when she looked in the peephole she saw a young man in a hotel uniform. He knocked again, a little louder this time.

"Ma'am, I'm here to assist you downstairs."

Deirdre opened the door and observed that this young man seemed casual and even younger than she'd expected. But now,

190

even someone 25 could seem so young to her. She had really aged in the last year.

The escort, whose name tag read CURTIS, smiled at her, took her by the arm, and they walked carefully and slowly to the exit, the stairwell, with its glass windows looking down on palms and tropical plants. She didn't bother with any small talk, and she barely paid attention to his polite banter. It was just chatter in her ears.

"Maybe on the way back," she said, "we can take the elevator."

"Of course, Miss," he said, with a professional politeness that she found reassuring.

When they came to the bottom of the stairwell and Curtis opened the door into the lobby, Deirdre felt like she might faint and held on tighter to his arm with her other hand. "You okay, Ma'am? Maybe you should sit down now?"

"Yes, I'll sit right over there, next to him." She pointed to where a tall man with a noticeable scar parted the hair on his head. He had a tattoo on his forearm, a wave. *Sean*, she thought. He stood waiting calmly but with a smile on his face. Curtis helped her walk over to an overstuffed chair, thick cotton with a subtle pattern of tropical leaves on the material. *She couldn't help noticing anything that had a plant on it,* Deirdre thought, beginning to relax a little.

Sean waited until the escort had helped Deirdre sit down and then asked, "Okay now?"

"Yes, Curtis, thank you. I'm fine." Sean got out of his chair and walked over closer as the young man left.

"Erin?" he asked. "Cleo," she said, "Cleo Green."

"Yes," Sean," said, "that's right, Cleo Green," Sean nodded and sat down in the matched chair next to her and put out his hand as if to shake.

"I'm sorry, Sean, I can't touch you right now, my hands are not very steady, and it's awkward for me. I hope you can understand."

191

"Yes, I can, and I do understand. I feel pretty nervous myself. But more importantly, I'm so relieved to see you in person, and I want to prove who I am by this bit, all that the desert had left for me, of the pink paisley scarf you had on that day in the desert. Do you want to see it?" He started to reach into his jacket pocket.

"No," she said louder than she meant to, "No, I do not want to see anything that had to do with that desert, nothing at all, and I believe you are who you say you are."

Sean felt like someone had struck him in the gut. After all his troubles to keep the bit of scarf, after being sure he'd need it, after thinking about this moment for so long, she did not wish to see it. His small secret treasure. Then he did everything he had learned to calm down, to try to understand things from the other person's point of view. Finally, his breathing steadied, and he was able to look up again and look at her face.

Tears were coming down, a slow trickle that she didn't bother to wipe away. He felt himself tear up too. And he had to look away for a minute to compose himself, to tell her what he and Mateo had agreed and what was next for this damaged woman. He would still keep the piece of scarf. Some day she may want it. He needed it, too, to remind himself of his act of courage. Anyway he had found a new pink paisley scarf for her and had it wrapped in a special gift box. MaeAnn had helped with that.

"Do I understand you then, that you do not wish to discuss the desert, any of it?"

"How it was lucky I saw you because I was driving slow and you had no clothes on and..."

"Stop, no more Sean, please, I guess I really can't handle it." Deirdre looked around the lobby to see if anyone had heard Sean. No one seemed at all interested in them.

Sean laid out a plan that he had made with Mateo in Long Beach. "My fiancee, MaeAnn and I will look after your place. We will keep it going for you while you are gone. We will get rid of any unwanted guests."

"Now, one more thing. Mateo will call you soon and he will tell you the rest of the plan. It includes a friend of mine from the Marine Corps, Rhonda. Just call her Rondi—she will be traveling with you. You will like her...everybody does."

Deirdre felt slightly confused, but she concentrated on the part where Mateo would call her soon. They had their phones, flip phones, hard to trace. It was all going to work out, and for some reason, she felt more and more comfortable with this man Sean, and confident in his plan and his ways. He promised her that he would not let anything happen to her. Deirdre thought that when Sean said this and he nodded his head as he was saying it, he almost seemed like a shaman. *He might start a chant*, she thought, *might nod along as he said a prayer over a smoking pot of sag*e. Deirdre shook her head and looked into his eyes.

"But will you watch over my Matalija poppies and take out and braid my garlic?" They both laughed at this, and he said, "Yes, my MaeAnn has a green thumb. I don't. We're getting married soon."

Deirdre found herself smiling as she stood and finally shook his big firm hand. "I'm happy for you Sean."

"Thanks, he said. Best thing that every happened to me so far," Sean said as he waved Curtis, who stood waiting by the reception desk, over. When Curtis held out his arm to Deirdre, Sean handed Curtis a package.

"This is for Miss Green. Would you carry it up for her?"

"Oh Sean, that is so thoughtful. I owe my life to you, and that, saving me, is the biggest gift you could ever have given me. Thank you!" She let Curtis take the box, though; it seemed too awkward to turn the gift down. When she nodded to him, Curtis reached over and took the box.

She held out her trembling hand to Sean once more, and he took it in his. Then she and Curtis turned and headed toward the elevator. "If there are people in the elevator, I must wait for an empty one," she said to Curtis, and he nodded. As she stepped into the empty elevator, she looked over her shoulder.

Sean was still standing there, like some sort of dark angel. He waved, but she did not wave back. She stepped into the elevator. Curtis looked out of the glass windows and Deirdre did the same.

She'd heard a message come in on her phone in her purse. After thanking Curtis, she walked over and tapped three times on Jimmy's door. She opened her room, then closed and locked her door and sat to take the message. It was from her sister.

I'm thinking about you and your trip. Mateo called me. I want to wish you safe travels and to say that I love you. Stay in touch.

Your sister, Lizzie.

This was enough to unleash tears. Deirdre dabbed at her eyes with a Kleenex, took a drink of water, and sat down in a chair to carefully open the wrapped box. Tissue paper rustled as she took the gift out and lifted it up. A pink paisley scarf, a new one carefully picked as a twin to the one she lost in the desert. She paused for a moment to admire the cloth, the paisley design and then carefully boxed it back up and set it by the trash can in the room. *Good for a maid or whoever wants it. I want to see nothing like it ever again*, she thought. At that, she lay down on her bed to rest for the journey ahead.

Chapter 39
Her Answer Is Yes

MaeAnn lay propped up in her bed. She needed this moment of solitude in her own space, in her own bed, with the covers pulled up. Why? Because she had just been proposed to, and she had said "yes."

MaeAnn still couldn't believe it. Sean had asked her to marry him. She, with her Tagalog language and a father in the military who was stationed in Hawaii when she was born. Part Philippines, part Hawaii, and part the rest of the world. Sean already knew she spoke Tagalog, and he could even repeat a few words back to her. She thought about her family's brief and cold stay in North Dakota with relatives who soon grew tired of their presence.

She took another sip of coffee remembering how she, her sister, and their parents had not been prepared for the snow drifts and the chilling winds. Eventually, her parents decided to move to California, where her father would be near a military base, Camp Pendleton, and her mother could enjoy growing her special onions and tomatoes. MaeAnn trusted Sean and she could tell him anything. She had told him that she had taken other women, as lovers in the past, and he seemed unfazed by it. Sean was unlike anyone she had met before, and she felt completely comfortable with him.

She knew that Sean carried emotional scars from both war and his childhood, just as she carried her own baggage. Her family had experienced disappointments, and she and her sister got occasional whippings when her father was drunk. Despite being good at waitressing, MaeAnn didn't define herself by that role. What truly made her feel alive was the feel of earth in her hands, poking seeds into holes and nurturing plants in a greenhouse. *I guess I am more like my Mom than I knew,* MaeAnn thought, throwing off the covers and stepping out of bed.

As she pulled on her cotton robe and slid into her flip flops she thought about surfing yesterday. How she really was getting it. She could successfully ride in all the way. The feeling she got while riding the waves made the ocean a second home for her. That was thanks to Sean and his patient teaching. She poured some cereal in a bowl and added fresh strawberries and half and half. As she ate, she imagined their future together. Her life with Sean.

When they married, she planned to teach him how to garden so they could grow their own vegetables. As for children, neither of them were entirely certain. They agreed to make that decision later on. Sean felt he was becoming too old to be a father, but he was willing to go along with it if MaeAnn really wanted kids. MaeAnn like kids well enough, but she had seen how friends seem to lose a part of themselves when they became moms. *Well,* she thought, *I don't have to think about this right now. What I have to do is get ready to be a bride, and to tell my friends and family about Sean's proposal.*

Sean had made a promise to her that convinced her to accept him as her husband. "You are the one for me, and I know you will never hurt me the way I've been hurt before. And I promise to never hurt you. I may not always be the most social guy, but I will be faithful and I will be honest. You will always be my top priority in everything I do."

Those were powerful words he had spoken, words she had never heard from any of her other loves. He was truly a different kind of man. He was the one for her. As she opened the curtains to see fog retreating, and the blue sky returning she imagined herself wearing a thick bundle of Hawaiin leis, and she heard Sean say to her, "*Ikaw Na Nga.*" And she would answer him with the same Tagalog words, *he was the one.* Then her mother and father would both cry, and her sister would hug her tight.

MaeAnn smiled as she pulled on shorts and her waitressing T-shirt. She brushed her hair back and carefully braided it, then put

196

on her thick soled waitressing shoes. She wondered if anyone would notice anything different about her today. She laughed out loud. Her day had begun.

Chapter 40
Every Rock and Leaf

Sean soared through the skies, embodying the raven in the photograph, diligently guarding his collection of sticks and cloth scraps for his nest.

In Sean's dream, he saw two men, both dressed in black, sitting together in a steel-walled room. Transforming into the crow-man, Sean flew into the room, dropping sticks and rocks on them until they toppled over and tumbled out of the space like pins in a bowling alley. "Rocks!" Sean exclaimed in his sleep, startling MaeAnn, who shook him until he settled down.

The following morning, as MaeAnn took the coffee cup Sean handed her she asked, "Why Rocks? Last night, what were you dreaming Sean?"

"I don't really remember, but someow it had to do with the one prayer my Paiute mother repeated to me when I was a kid. On her rare visits, she would say it to me as she was getting ready to leave, and it always made me feel better."

"I'd like to hear it, Sean."

"Oh, Great Spirit, Let me walk in Beauty.
Let me learn the lessons in every rock and leaf.
When life fades, let me come to you without shame. "

Sean looked over at MaeAnn who stood up, and came over to him.

She wrapped her arms around him, planted a kiss on his cheek, and remarked, "That is simply beautiful, Sean. It's a gift from your troubled mother that carries something good."

"And you, MaeAnn, are my something good," Sean replied, their smiles widening, soon transforming into laughter for no particular reason. The timer on the stove clicked off with a loud *ding.* MaeAnn walked over, opened the oven door, and pulled out a blueberry lemon loaf glazed with lime marmalade.

Sean's kitchen smelled citrusy like the lemon groves he had played in as a kid when he visited his foster cousins in Riverside. Sean thought to himself, *Life is damn good,* as he playfully patted MaeAnn on her bottom and flashed a broad smile. "Looks delicious," he said.

"It still needs to cool," she said..

"Damn, you know me too well," Sean chuckled, shaking his head. "How did I get so lucky to fall in love with a lovely lady who bakes!" Although he knew that the sweet loaf might crumble, he still wanted a taste right away. He liked it best when just out of the oven. Sean fetched two small plates and two forks, giving MaeAnn a pleading look. "You look just like my old dog, begging for something from the table," MaeAnn said, caressing Sean's face. "Of course, you're cuter than my pet dog, and I love you even more. Just five more minutes, and then we can sit and enjoy our cake together."

Sean opened the front door and walked outside to listen for morning sounds; the beach was waking up too. He was greeted by loud wingbeats of pelicans and shrill cries of seagulls, along with the soothing lapping of small waves. The rhythmic sounds of the sea always relaxed Sean, and he closed his eyes for a minute. Today the sea lions and seals were quiet. The fog was retreating and he could hear a foghorn off in the distance. After stretching, he came back inside. "You are truly remarkable, you know that," he said. "I love you so much, MaeAnn."

"I know," she replied, cutting two generous slices and placing them on the table. "I know."

Sean felt completely satisfied. Waking up with MaeAnn and sharing their morning together. This was how it was going to be. This is what he could look forward to now. She turned toward him and asked, "Well, what do you think. Is this lemony bread a good one." "Excellent," he said, "and I think I have to have another piece right now."

199

MaeAnn laughed and passed the plate over to Sean. Like Sean and sweets, *I just can't get enough of this man*, she thought, as she finished her coffee. *Life is sweet today.*

Chapter 41
Paz y Bien

Deirdre strolled along Montevideo beach, relishing the calm before afternoon winds stirred. She smiled as she looked at her footprints, steps sinking into the sand, noticing how her stride now appeared confident instead of a disorganized hobble.

At the start of the trip, Deirdre had been exhausted. The meeting with Sean in Newport Beach, followed by the hurried flights from John Wayne Airport to Mexico and then to Uruguay, had left her dazed. She was slowly recovering here.

Sean, the heroic man, promised to take care of her Matilija poppies, Mexican tube roses, and garlic. He had promised that the plants would be thoroughly watered during the summer. *The summer season, which seemed hotter now than it was a few years ago,* she thought. Deirdre anticipated the delightful scents in the garden that would greet her upon her return to Long Beach. She imagined their expansive garden in California, moon vine plant winding across the back fence. Of course, she thought, no one could care for their home gardens like Mateo. He had a meticulous approach and a natural way with plants.

Following Mateo's instructions, Sean had a security firm install an alarm for times when he couldn't be there. *Everything seemed settled,* Deirdre thought. They would remain in Uruguay for as long as they needed and wanted to. *She could let go of her worries.*

Deirdre waved as she spotted Arguello with his boogie board. He waved back to her, while Teo and his parents sat in the sand talking. She turned and headed in the opposite direction, a routine all of them had become accustomed to as she walked — back and forth—over and over. *They didn't consider it strange any more,* she thought.

Deirdre remembered the trip down here. Rhonda, Sean's friend and another ex-Marine, had met her at the hotel. Jimmy waited until the two women walked to the plane bound for Mexico. Rhonda turned out to be bigger and more muscular than Deirdre had expected, but Deirdre immediately sensed she could rely on her to help her leave the country. Deirdre traveled with just a small carry-on, wearing a wig and hoping it wouldn't cause too much discomfort. Rhonda sat beside her on the plane as they flew to Mexico to meet Mateo.

During the flight, Deirdre experienced spells of quiet crying. Rhonda gently tapped her shoulder each time and offered the same comforting words, "It's all right, let it out, honey."

Deirdre kept seeing a sterile room with dim lighting, tubes attached to her wrists, and then she remembered running down a hallway with her pink scarf trailing behind. There were fragmented glimpses of driving and being followed, a forced veer off the road, and a syringe piercing her arm through her clothes. After that, nothing until she woke up in a hospital room. These images replayed over and over until she had eventually fallen into a deep sleep, with the jet engines' whirring like the purring of a colossal cat. It was hard to let go of these images, these memories.

Deirdre began a slow jog. It felt good as the breeze had picked up and cooled her off.

She remembered that Rhonda spoke to her, rousing her from a nap as as the plane landed in Punta del Este, where Mateo awaited their arrival. "Mateo," Rhonda said, "He will be here."

Deirdre looked at Rhonda and said it once again, "Mateo."

"That's right, your man will be here for you," Rhonda had chuckled quietly. Deirdre now knew that Rhonda had a wife and children—two daughters and a son—in Los Angeles. As she walked the beach, Deirdre remembered that she had hated to leave Rhonda, even if she was meeting Teo.

"Don't you worry now, I'm not going anywhere until you have your bag and are safely with Mateo," Rhonda assured her, wrapping an arm around her. It was as if she had read Deirdre's thoughts.

Deirdre stopped to catch her breath and when she saw her husband on the sand she thought about how happy she had been to see him at the airport in Mexico. They had both hugged Rhonda as she turned to wait for a plane back to California.

Deirdre walked back to where Teo and his parents sat. They had a family resemblance that she had never really noticed before now. Especially her husband and his mother. Here they were Teo, Arguello and herself. They were tucked in with Teo's family, in Uruguay, enjoying the tranquility of the morning on the soft sands. They planned to stay here in Uruguay for a few months, waiting on the outcome of legal matters: injunctions, court dates, and restraining orders—all part of the pursuit of justice. *Stay here as long as we want to,* Deirdre repeated to herself.

Her husband took her hands, and Deirdre felt an immense sense of relief as he pulled her into a warm embrace. In this moment, here in Uruguay, Teo made her feel loved and secure. She was growing her dark blond hair, intending to tie it back in a ponytail whenever she was strong enough to go swimming again.

"Don't think about anything, Deirdre Erin, just be here with me, breathing in the sea air. Tonight, we'll enjoy some delicious shrimp. Look at our son; he's so happy here, and he is fluent in Spanish. Now he wants to learn some indigenous words. Mother isn't entirely sure about that," they both laughed, embracing each other. Deirdre experienced a calmness that had eluded her for months.

She would be fine. She wanted to explore the uses of sacred moon vine with a legitimate, ethically-minded group that respected the traditional uses of the plant, and the people who had been using the plant for years. Then she could move on to something else. Or perhaps she would simply relish tending their extensive vegetable garden and watching her son play soccer. She wanted to spend more time with her sister and her sister's growing baby boy, Bahar. Deirdre liked Bahar's father, Najid, but suspected he had some hidden agenda. He had briefly mentioned being in hiding himself and expressed a desire to see changes in Iran, which, in his mind, was still Persia. She needed to be around him to get a sense of who he really was.

****

Deirdre and Mateo sat outside on a star-filled Montevideo night. "Tell me everything you can remember about that last trip. It will be good for you," Mateo said, taking a bite of tamale from a big platter of food brought to them by the house cook. Deirdre dipped a shrimp into some spicy pepper sauce and began to talk about her most recent trip to Paraguay—the trip that led to everything that happened afterwards and brought her to where she sat now, looking out at the sea with her husband.

Deirdre recalled stopping to tie the lace of her boot, which was different from the sandals she wore on her first visit. She remembered watching a harmless snake slither into the bushes. "Teo, there were so many more farms this time—some growing yerba mate, some with acres of fruit trees, and others higher up with lots of cattle. But I also saw a couple of bright wild orchids and a small herd of deer grazing on wild grasses. The volcano had just a couple of little puffs coming up."

"I walked directly towards the shaman's house. I felt like my hiking boots wouldn't let anything unexpected sting or bite me, that no roots would trip me, and that no one would harm me. I wouldn't let anyone harm this place or these people," Deirdre said, as Mateo smiled and nodded.

"That shaman is old now; the people say he's a hundred years old. He smudged me and blessed me, and then he said, 'Keep your eyes and ears open. Don't go the usual ways, become a panther, take another path.' I wasn't sure what he really meant." Deirdre paused for a sip of her iced mescal drink before continuing.

She lowered her head, trying to recall more details for her husband and herself. "The path was more overgrown than I remembered, and I had to watch my step. A recent earthquake had

204

crumbled a few of the stone walls on the way to the ruins, but the ruins themselves remained much the same as they were fourteen years ago. The faded tiles, the walls covered in vines, and even the woman's head—someone had cleaned around her with a straw broom. The look on her face was still disconcerting, even more so than the first time. Back then, I was younger and full of life, unafraid and eager for adventure. I wanted to experience magic," Deirdre recounted.

"You did," Mateo said, taking another bite of tamale. "You experienced magic."

"When I went around the corner away from the woman's head, there was something scratched into the wall where a big tree had toppled and taken a part of the wall with it. It was an image— a flower, a circle with a cross inside, and the words *paz y bien.*" She gave Mateo an intent look. It was something he had taught her and Arguello to say, a special phrase for their family instead of goodbye. He always said it to her when she embarked on a journey. P*az y bien.*

"I think it sounds like the people drew what they saw inside that blossom of the moon vine. And they all say *paz y bien.* I know it's special to our family, but it is a common way to say hello and goodbye, go in peace and goodwill," Mateo said, giving her a big smile.

"It has been fourteen years, Teo. Do you remember the pictures I sent you from my phone?" Deirdre asked.

"Yes," Mateo replied quietly. "I have them on a thumb drive hidden at home in Long Beach."

"The vine blossom was vibrant with its strong orange color and pink striations, with a circle and a cross shape inside. Before my phone disappeared in all that desert mess," Deirdre continued. She started to shake, and Mateo moved closer, putting his arm around her. "Just tell me as much as you remember, as much as you want to tell me."

"Well, the tea I made there was very strong, and I don't remember much except intense colors and the feeling of being at one with the plants, the surroundings, even the birds and the big lizard crossing the broken tiles. I saw myself as a jaguar. It all fit together perfectly, like giant pieces of a jigsaw puzzle. Slowly, I came back to normal and felt disappointed because so much vibrancy had disappeared."

"Then I hiked back the way I had come and nodded to the woman and the shaman, who was sitting outside smoking a pipe of something. It was an incredible journey, much like the first."

"You are here, and the people of the ruins in Paraguay are fine, and the plant is safe. There's no need to share this with anyone. It's enough that the people there know it, and protect it. So, you see, now you can forget about it."

"I know that's good advice, my Teo, thank you," Deirdre said. Deirdre finished her cool drink. She knew she couldn't forget, but she would first find a way to propagate the plant locally in California. Then she would find an ethical group to use it for good. She shook her head and nodded once again to her husband.

Mateo took her hands in his. "I love you and honor you. Stay right here with me, right now. Try not to imagine anything else. You have a lot of guardians now."

But even as she smiled at him, she knew that the scent of the flower and the visions would always be with her. For now, she agreed with him, shaking her head 'yes' as she leaned in to kiss him, their kisses tasting of the sea and red chili peppers.

Epilogue

Najid was teaching Bahar a few Farsi words. Elizabeth looked at Najid. He had a smile on his face as Bahar sputtered, trying to copy him, but the words came out jumbled. *At one year old, Bahar was a bright little guy and was going to be a talker,* Elizabeth thought. Finally, he covered his ears and then reached out to Najid, saying clearly, "Up."

So far, she was enjoying this little boy and she realized that the more he talked and was exerting his independence the more she really enjoyed her time with him. Najid was smitten with his son and he was happy to take Bahar any time Elizabeth needed some free time. But Najid still traveled and he wasn't around all the time. Still, he was a good dad and that is all she cared about She couldn't believe how much her life had changed over the last two years of Najid and Bahar. She felt a more clear sense of purpose now, and the work on her thesis was progressing. She didn't miss her little Vespa because Najid had gotten a bicycle and the two of them rode paths with Bahar in a little cart behind them. It was a very different life now.

There's no stopping him, Elizabeth thought. Their little Bahar. Boy of springtime and of the sea. Elizabeth wrapped herself in her pashmina, the pink one, and went over to sit next to her son and his father. She felt a certain sense of peace and contentment. She would even say, she felt happy.

******

It was their wedding day, and when she turned to look at Sean. he noticed the colorful batch of flowers MaeAnn had chosen, some from her mother's garden and some from Deirdre and Mateo's place. He shook, just a little, getting tearful, but then the minister pronounced them married. He heard himself let out a loud, "Whoopee!" And as he did, MaeAnn tossed her bouquet up into the air, the sea breeze capturing it and tumbling it down to the

207

water. No one really noticed because the couple was busy kissing while the guests tossed rose petals, which rained down upon them.

MaeAnn and Sean walked hand in hand into the ocean just up to their knees, getting their wedding clothes wet. Then they kissed and kissed some more. A small group that included Sean's sister and his foster brother, MaeAnn's family, and some of her best friends from the restaurant, and his from the beach, applauded the couple. As requested, Sean's two gallery owners took phone photos. When the couple turned to come back up the beach for a small party, a seal from a nearby rock began barking, loud and funny. "Seal of approval," Sean quipped as guests clapped and laughed again.

He leaned down and took MaeAnn's hand in his. *Nothing more is needed,* he thought.

******

Smoke swirled above the shaman's head as he waved the bundle of burning sage sticks over the backs of the village couple. Pottery shards were scattered about, mixed into volcanic debris. The chanting was in Spanish, low and soothing. The couple sat still, quiet, and intent in a place swept clean with a corn bristle broom. Deirdre noticed that they didn't mind the dirt or the noise of a group of hikers below. They were being blessed before their wedding. The wedding would be later. in the Catholic church, but this was as important to them.

Then the tea was sipped, and the couple lay down together, holding each other tightly. The woman's embroidered blouse seemed to quiver with color in the late afternoon sun. The shaman sipped some tea and then turned to face the sharp peak of the volcano. His skin was wrinkled, but he looked regal. He started chanting again, this time not in Spanish but in an ancient tongue. *The old ways survive despite everything,* Deirdre thought as she smiled, then turned to go.

She said a silent prayer. And then quietly, as she started her walk down, she softly said, "*paz y bien.*"

She held her hands against her heart and said something more.

"Thank you for this sacred place."

The springtime of Lovers has come,
that this dust bowl may become a garden;
the proclamation of heaven has come,
that the bird of the soul may rise in flight.

The sea becomes full of pearls,
the salt marsh becomes sweet as kauthar,
the stone becomes a ruby from the mine,
the body becomes wholly soul.

Mewlana Jalaluddin Rumi.

210

Acknowledgements

Members of PILS writing group: Barbara Baer, Robin Beeman, Mary Gaffney, Andrea Granahan, Liza Prunuske and (the late) Susan Swartz. Thank you for your patient listening, and your suggestions to make this book happen.

Beta Readers: Bob Burnett, Roger Collins, Patrick Fanning, Sara Peyton, Roger House.

Cover Design: Sadira Attebery and *The Urban Book Publishers* design team.

Thanks to my family and friends.

I especially thank my husband Roger House for his consistent enthusiasm for this project, for his diligence in copy editing, suggesting, and sage technical support.

Author, Marylu Downing welcomes your comments and questions. If you want discussion topics for a book group reading of this book, please go to the website: **moonvinesbooks.com** for more about *Pink Paisley Scarf:*

Made in the USA
Middletown, DE
17 April 2024

53179052R00124